Miami Fire

By
RICK MURCER

PUBLISHED BY:
Murcer Press, LLC

Edited by
Janet Fix, www.thewordverve.com

Interior book design by
Bob Houston eBook Formatting

www.rickmurcer.com

Miami Fire © 2015 Rick Murcer
All rights reserved

This book is a work of fiction. The names, characters, places, and incidents are products of the writer's imagination or have been used fictitiously and are not to be construed as real. Any resemblance to persons, living or dead, actual events, locales or organizations is entirely coincidental.

ISBN: 0692420541

For JC, who loves me and keeps me on the path, eternally.

Miami Fire

A Novel

By
RICK MURCER

CHAPTER-1

Manny Williams sprinted around the street corner into the dark, rancid alley, never missing a stride, his feet adjusting to the worn brick as his eyes searched and his ears strained for the telltale clue.

There it was.

The echo of the pathetic weasel's footfalls, accompanied by his faint, harsh breathing, was heading away from Manny on his left, toward the abandoned riverfront buildings.

Predictable. Idiots were always predictable.

The target's fear-ridden attempt at escape only served to spur Manny further. Paybacks are great motivators, and this dick would find out what that meant.

His training as a special agent for the FBI had added to his physical stamina, but that wasn't really on his mind. Not now. It didn't need to be. He would run a marathon to catch this one.

The face of the wiry man with the close-set eyes and stringy hair was all he could distinguish through his anger. The worthless punk had raised a knife to Manny's family. No one did that. No one.

Manny ran faster.

Taking time to sort things out, to compartmentalize so that he didn't react irrationally to situations like he'd experienced moments ago, had always been a strength for him, but he ignored any pretense of that skill for the moment. This asshole was going to pay for threatening his wife and son.

Pay dearly.

Four more strides into the alley, then a quick left, and he suddenly made out the poor excuse for a human being, dressed in jeans and faded Army jacket, through the semi-light of dusk. He was moving close to the decrepit red brick wall of the abandoned apartment building, trying to stay out of Manny's view and away from his determination to find him by hugging the shadows.

Heaven or hell couldn't have prevented Manny from getting to him now.

Turning one step to the exact angle he'd need to intercept him, Manny kicked into another gear and sprinted directly toward the perp's hopeful exit at the chain-linked fence between the two rundown buildings.

As Manny cleared the sight line of the first building, he saw the weasel climbing the tall rusted gate that would lead him out of Manny's reach and sprinting toward the Grand River.

Manny smiled. The pathetic ass would never make it over that fence.

A few seconds later, Manny had almost reached the gate.

"Get down from there, asshole. Come take your medicine," he yelled.

"Get bent." The weasel snarled, but Manny could hear the fear.

The perp then twisted in Manny's direction, making a throwing motion.

The glint from the blade was warning enough as Manny hurled himself out of the path of the knife, rolling along the uneven alley floor.

His anger exploded.

He leaped up and made the fence just as the piece of garbage started to swing himself over.

Manny grabbed his left leg, wrenched hard to the right, heard something snap, and then yanked with all of his strength. The man screamed and then thumped ungraciously to the ground.

Humpty-Dumpty had a great fall.

"You . . . you broke my leg," he screamed. "You broke it."

"Did I? I bet that hurts like hell. Let me check it out."

"No! Don't touch me. You need to call 911."

Manny could see that his wife's attacker's pain was now joined by more fear. It should be. As he started to scoot away, Manny put his foot on the man's chest.

"Like I said, I think you need to let me look at it first. So stay where you are, got it?"

He nodded his head in rapid succession. "O-okay, Man, just don't hurt me again."

Manny dropped to his knees, inches from the crooked nose of his wife's and child's assailant. The man's breath reeked of sour wine, his eyes bloodshot and lost.

"Hurt you? You pulled a knife on a woman carrying a baby and demanded cash or you'd cut the kid, *my* kid. My son. What should I do with a scumbag who would do that?"

"I wouldn't have—"

He didn't finish his sentence before Manny slapped him.

The sound resonated throughout the alley.

"You wouldn't have what? Cut them, or worse?"

"Stop, Please. No, I swear, man. I just need money for booze. That's all."

"So you rob innocent women and children because you need to get drunk?"

Manny drew back his hand to hit him again as all of the hell his family had endured over the last few weeks rose to the very top of his emotions.

His daughter Jen had shot a man who had been stalking Manny's mother-in-law, Haley Rose. The crazy shit was intending to kill Jen, his son Ian, and Haley Rose, if he didn't get what he wanted. Jen had had no choice. He admired her for doing what it took, but no seventeen-year-old should have to live with that, ever.

He could see Jen's eyes, still, as she told him that pulling that trigger had been the worst, but she'd do it again to save her brother and her granny. No doubt she would. He loved her for her strength but hated the scar that might be on her soul for the rest of her life. Now this low-life had threatened to take away two of the great joys in his life with an eight-inch blade.

To put a cherry on top of these events, why in the name of God couldn't he take a vacation without running into the sickest of the sick and almost get himself or his staff killed in the process? Why was that so much to ask?

He was tired of all of it. Being a profiler and seeing what he routinely saw was difficult enough, but this situation was screwing with his down time, his family time, and that was intolerable. The frustration burned inside like nothing he'd experienced in years. Maybe ever.

No more. Someone was going to pay. This shithead would do just fine.

He cocked his fist back farther, his eyes on fire, and began to bring it down to mash this perp's face into the bricks . . . then held it.

Then what, Williams? What are you then? You become what you swore to protect against? You take revenge, justified or not, just because you can?

There existed a fine line between justice and revenge, and no one knew that better than he. Even so, Manny had been prepared to step over that line in the name of his family. Yet, in the end, if he did, what truly separated him from those who had to be taken off the streets?

This Guardian of the Universe persona, his daughter's nickname for him, wasn't always all it was cracked up to be, but it was the right one.

The man flinched as Manny brought his hand down and tweaked his nose, albeit a bit too hard.

"Ouch. What are you doing?"

"Not beating the shit out of you. This is your lucky day. You'll get to go to jail without going to see a plastic surgeon first."

"Whatever. I'm already in bad shape. I need something for my pain."

Manny didn't answer. He lifted the man from the alley floor and slung him over his shoulder.

"What are you doing? I need to get to a hospital. I can't feel my ankle."

"I left my cell in the car, so I'll have to carry you until we get to a phone. And don't think about doing something stupid, or I will toss your ass in the river."

"You're nuts, man. Who in hell are you?"

Manny thought that was a good question.

CHAPTER·2

It hadn't really been that difficult, had it? Nothing for him truly could be classified as difficult since his real awakening. There had been a few attempts at releasing the real genius, but nothing like this. He was now totally without chains of any kind.

It was genuinely remarkable how freeing it was when one finally came to grips with his true lot in life, his purpose. He doubted many ever reached the pinnacle that was his to cherish, but then again, he'd sought it out while most accepted their miserable, mundane lives the way they unfolded. He'd made the difficult choice of not settling for ordinary, and it was a grand decision indeed . . . because it was about what he could do for others. That was the key, and he'd opened the door with it.

Taking three steps forward, he reached out his hand to caress his creation. And it was his, make no mistake.

He frowned. Creation? He supposed some would see it that way, but that would mean he'd had a selfish purpose for creating it, yes? That was not the case. He only indulged in these joyous activities because he wanted to be faithful to his role in this life's drama while giving the people what they so desperately wanted.

Tilting his head, taking in the whole of his surrounds, he believed he was getting there, that his journey was far closer to the end than the beginning.

For him, there were no hidden agendas from his past that caused him to seek this path. No abusive, horny, overbearing mother. No screwed-up old man who slept with his sister or bent him over at will. No huddling in a corner after an uncle performed some unspeakable act on him or some priest had his way with him.

In fact, his upbringing and kin and even his church had been far more normal than many. He'd even had a couple of dogs, and he'd possessed no desire to harm them. He'd never wet the bed, and fire was simply fire to him. Well, almost.

He didn't mind when a match got too close to his fingers; and his gold-plated, customized lighter had its own uses, but he was far from obsessed with flames.

There was no deep religious conviction espousing sinful man's war against good, no voices from the devil or God Himself. There was no tragic—what did the shrinks call it?—psychotic episode or life-altering event that had snapped his precarious grip on reality and sent him careening down this path.

Hell, he'd never even been jilted by a lover, causing his hazardous perch on sanity to tumble down into oblivion and meet with the dark side. Even though he didn't really date often, he had enjoyed a woman's company more than once, the touching of flesh on flesh. Just not nearly as much as the other kind of touching, he guessed.

There had been one incident that helped him release his inner understanding, but that had been far from traumatic.

The truth of the matter was that he was born to do what he did.

It was like a writer or an athlete or a sailor or a carpenter who knew from some early age their calling had been decreed. It was simply instinctive, a gifted perception for the vocation that nature bestowed upon those who recognized their individual gift and embraced it.

Uncomplicated, unpretentious.

His acceptance of this destiny wasn't the end of the story, rather the beginning.

He desired to excel, to be the very best, and more so, to compare himself with others. To humbly accept the accolades, to hear unmatched praise for raising his game to the highest level, was paramount.

What could be better than practicing one's destined vocation and being considered the most accomplished at the same time?

Perhaps law enforcement wouldn't view it that way. He was no fool. He understood his act of service wouldn't exactly be greeted with platitudes of admiration. The police would want to end him, probably in more ways than one.

His service went stiffly against the laws of men, but not the laws of nature. He knew that now. Still, he would have to watch his ass, as they say. There weren't many better at that, either.

The warm southern Florida breeze hurried over his face, rustling his dark hair as he reached out his hand once again, running his forefinger down the other side. Even in the still of the late night, he saw clearly what was next.

So smooth, so warm, so much potential to satisfy and be a monument for this man's own sake.

There was a slight flutter in his chest. His anticipation began to crescendo. Yet, what he was experiencing was more than enthusiasm or excitement. Fulfillment was a far superior ideal.

"I've waited for this. I truly have. While there is nothing in it specifically for you in this life, you will be forever remembered. Sometimes life isn't balanced the way we wish, but in the end, you'll get yours."

His fingers grasped the blonde hair of the young man bound to the large magnolia tree. He gently raised his head. The man's breath reeked of a coppery metallic scent that he'd grown to readily recognize. He supposed he should have anticipated the stink when he'd removed the man's tongue with his new tin snips, but he'd been concentrating far more on the act than any residual effects.

"Chalk up another lesson to experience," he said softly.

The man began to moan as his eyes refocused.

Interesting. A desperate plea registered in his captive's eyes; yet, there was a trace of resignation as well. He understood. He suspected he might have gone down that road himself, especially after he'd lost ears and all ten fingers, never mind the series of long incisions running from his liver toward his heart.

The pain must be unimaginable; yet sacrifice was the fuel that burned the flame of fame.

Reaching into the belt of his black cargo shorts, he pulled out the third knife, the nine-inch blade that could easily shave the toughest of beards, and placed it in his left hand.

"It is time," he said. "And, when it is over for you, I promise to take the same great care with your wife. You are both truly special."

Moving patiently, his eyes fixated on the knife and the hand wielding it, he went to work, beginning just below the lower abdominal wall and moving slowly up. He then fixed on the man's face. Twenty minutes later, after spending a few more moments admiring his giftedness and the young man's legacy, he patiently circled the tree and then took the hand of the gagged young woman who was now a widow.

"I'm sorry that I took so long with your husband. Take heart in the fact that he did well, but I've kept you waiting. It must be difficult to endure the idea of being married for only two nights before your honeymoon is over."

Bending to her, he kissed her on the forehead.

She shied away, eyes wide.

He stepped back and, this time, removed the two small knives from his belt.

"But the pain of that situation won't last too long compared to your everlasting reward. I promise. And I'm a man of my word."

The warm wind freshened again.

CHAPTER·3

"So why in hell didn't you call me or something? I could have used a little action too."

Manny smiled at Sophie Lee as she sat in the booth next to Dean Mikus, her husband of almost a year. The petite FBI special agent and Lucy Liu look-a-like had been his detective partner with the Lansing Police Department and now with the FBI for over twelve years.

She'd seen him through a tough time or two, including the errant gunshot death of his first wife, Louise, and the hell that came looking for him after that.

He'd seen Sophie through two divorces, a boob job, and a career change, and watched her fall deeply in love with the bearded man who'd courted her the minute he laid eyes on her at an airport in San Juan. What girl wouldn't fall for a guy who got down on his knee, kissed her hand, and called her the Queen of Everything?

She and Manny had history, no question, but he also recognized that tone in her voice for what it was. She really did enjoy the action of a good scrap, but what she was really saying was: *I'm glad you and Chloe and Ian are all right, and you should have killed the bastard. I would have.*

"My cell was still in the car. I didn't take it into the store. When I came out and saw that he was threatening Chloe and Ian with that knife, I yelled at him and he took off. I followed him . . . and the rest is history," said Manny.

"Do you think he really would have tried to hurt us?" asked Chloe, sliding a little closer to him, Ian sleeping on her lap.

Chloe Franson, now Chloe Williams, his redheaded wife, born and raised in Ireland and an ex-FBI special agent herself—who also happened to be a curvy bombshell and the head detective at the LPD—knew the answer to that. She wouldn't have allowed any such foolishness. Chloe would have throttled the killer or shot him through an eye before letting anything happen to Ian. Her temper was something not to trifle with. Manny knew that from experience.

"I think you would have denutted him first," said Sophie.

"I agree," said Dean.

"Yep, me too," said Manny.

"Dang, you four are harsh," said Alex Downs, grinning. "I think she would have used his intestines as a lasso."

Alex, a talented forensics expert and Dean's partner in that facet of the FBI's Behavioral Analysis Unit, was sitting directly across from Manny.

The balding, overweight man with the thick black glasses wore an expression that made him look like a candidate for the geek of the year award. But that look, and his appearance, belied his intellect and instinctive gift for crime scene analysis. He'd worked with Manny in Lansing for eight years before taking his talent to the Feds. There wasn't anyone better at that science/art than his long-time friend.

"Nice visual there, Alex. That makes it unanimous. Nutless and gutless in the same minute," said Dean, adjusting his green paisley driver's cap. "Never mess with a woman and her child, especially her first born."

The laughter from Manny's circle of friends caused him to laugh as well. He remembered what his old, deceased friend, Gavin Crosby, used to say.

No one ever laughed too much.

The crew grew silent and Manny knew what was coming next and who it would come from.

"So did you mean to break his ankle? I mean, I understand the slap, but I wasn't sure about the ankle," said Sophie, searching his face.

Running his hand through his hair, an old nervous habit from his childhood, Manny glanced around the booth.

Did he? Did he really know? All he knew was that Chloe never had the opportunity to defend herself and Ian. His elevated anger had made that protection a non-issue.

"That's a good question. I wrenched on his foot to get it loose from the chain-link fence, and then pulled him down. I may have had some intent. Who knows for sure if I don't?"

"The perp says you did it on purpose," said Chloe.

"Of course the piece of sh—errr, sorry, Ian— junk would say that. But you don't work for the LPD anymore, so it shouldn't be an issue," said Sophie.

"He's asleep," said Chloe, grinning. "And you're right about that. I suppose the FBI could sic the Office of Professional Responsibility on you, but they've got bigger fish to fry, don't ya know."

"I don't think the OPR cares much. But I don't think any of that's the real question," said Manny.

Sophie sighed. "I hate hanging around with savant profilers. You're right. The real question is: were you pissed and out of control enough to break the man's bones?"

There it was, the question that was on all of their minds, including his. The truth was he didn't really know.

Manny laid his hands on the table. "Maybe. All I could see when I was chasing him down was the rollercoaster Jen and I had ridden over the last few years, including losing Louise. Losing Gavin and the Casnovskys. Losing Max Tucker. That asshole Argyle flashing across my mind. What Chloe's mom had to endure with her ex, and Jen having to shoot a man to save her family, it was all too much, I suppose."

He fought for control as the thoughts kept coming, found it, and continued.

"How the senseless killing of innocent folks by screwed-up serial killers have messed up every vacation we've tried to take. Then how the good things in life have helped us to rebound only to have this low-life threaten to take it all away with a couple swipes of a butcher knife. It wasn't going to happen, that's all. *I* wasn't going to let it happen. Period. Not to us or anyone else."

He fought the urge to run his hand through his hair. "So, yes. I suppose I was in a rage, but I'm not sure of the out-of-control part. I mean, he's still alive, right?"

Chloe kissed him on the cheek.

"What was that for?"

"For keeping me out of prison. I probably would have killed him."

"I wondered if I might," said Manny.

"Hey, at least you could have gotten conjugal visits. I hear those trailers are pretty comfortable," said Sophie.

Alex shook his head. "I've asked this before, but I really have to know. Is that all you think about? Sex?"

"Nope, Dough Boy. I just like to bring it up because I'm pretty sure you ain't getting as much as me."

"What? Shows you what you know. And stop calling me Dough Boy."

"Always a treat with you two," said Chloe. "Anyway, big Frank Wymer questioned the attacker in the hospital. He confessed that you backed off and then tweaked his nose. Then you carried him to the corner to get a ride to the hospital."

"Did I?" asked Manny.

"You did. I saw the carrying part when I came to find you."

"You know what, Big Boy? No matter what you think about losing it a little, you kept yourself together better than the rest of us who have gone through less," said Sophie.

"She's right," said Alex. "Oh, shit. Did I just say that?"

"Can't take it back, Dough Boy. We all heard it," said Sophie.

"Damn that Dough Boy crap. Anyway, we get it, okay?" said Alex.

"Okay. Thanks, but let's let this go. I'm tired, and I want to have dessert before we go home," said Manny.

"Yeah, it'll be my last one for a couple of weeks," said Alex.

"Why? You going to lose fifty pounds?" asked Sophie.

"Bite me. No, as a matter of fact, the final approvals came down from Quantico to have my new bionic hand installed. Complete with the latest technology that we talked about before the shit went down in Las Vegas. I'm officially going to have the upgrade installed, so to speak, that I have been hoping for."

There was no wiping the smile from Alex's face. Even Sophie bit her tongue and had a certain spark of joy in her brown eyes. A true miracle when it came to the verbal sparring those two enjoyed.

Manny found himself relieved that the conversation had taken a different road. He'd spent enough time dwelling on his psyche.

"Well, it's about time. I couldn't be happier for you," said Chloe.

To put an exclamation point on her thoughts, she got up, handed Ian to Manny, and slid around the booth. She then kissed Alex on the forehead and gave him a heartfelt hug.

Manny felt the same happiness for Alex, and appreciation for the man. He had lost his hand defending Chloe, and she wouldn't be here if he hadn't. His good friend had been willing to sacrifice everything for the both of them.

This new hand wouldn't be like the real thing, but a geek like Alex had already researched the possibilities and was eagerly awaiting the opportunity to see what the Cadillac of prosthetic limbs could do.

His wife returned to his side.

"Aw, thanks, Chloe," Alex said softly. "That's way better than getting a hug from Williams."

"So which type of hand is it?" asked Dean, his own geek persona shining though his eyes.

"Well, we talked about a couple of them, but this one has a certain number of electrodes around some thin metal cuffs that actually interface with nerve fibers from my arm to my hand, called axons, and then they send electrical pulses between the two, enabling my hand to feel what my arm says it should. Another thing—" he stopped, smiling. "Okay. Okay. I won't bore you with the rest of this, but I'm looking forward to feeling things again. And I will, if this works."

"Yeah, your right hand must be getting tired," said Sophie.

Alex ignored her after a quick roll of his eyes.

"So when is the surgery?" asked Manny.

"I leave tomorrow for Walter Reed and I'll be out of commission for a couple of weeks."

He looked at Sophie.

"I'm bringing, Barb, you know, to make sure the hand works."

"Oh good God, man, even I don't want to deal with that image," said Sophie.

"Deal with it anyway."

More laughter circled the table.

After a few more minutes, Alex got up from the table. "I've got to go pack. The FBI's jet will be at the airport bright and early, and I don't want to miss that puppy."

"And we don't want you to," said Dean. "I want a full report when you can talk, okay?"

"You got it."

Alex shook hands with Manny and Dean, gave Sophie a hug, kissed Chloe, and disappeared around the corner into the late spring air of Michigan.

"What if we get a case when he's out?" said Sophie.

"We'll be fine. That's where Belle Simmons comes into play. She and Josh will have to help pick up the slack," said Manny.

Belle Simmons, the BAU's latest hire and maybe the most talented, had been great help on her first case when they were in Cozumel. She wasn't just a profiler, and a damned good one, but she also understood the forensic world almost as well as Alex and Dean. Add in her quirky taste in music and a few personal demons, and the Whitney Houston look-a-like was a perfect fit.

"Well, there's that. But hey, no cases yet, so maybe we can get some R and R to make up for the last shitty vacation we almost got to enjoy," said Sophie.

"I couldn't agree..."

Manny's phone vibrated in his jean's pocket. He took it out, read the ID, and answered.

"Hey Josh. Speak of the devil, we were just talking about you."

"I hope it was positive."

"No, we were wondering when we'd get a non-jerk for a boss."

"Funny boy. That ain't going to happen."

"Fair enough."

Josh grew serious. "You need to pack up the gang and meet Belle and me in Miami."

"A case, I assume?"

"Yeah, not a vacation, I'm afraid. A case it is. And not a normal one."

"We never have a normal one."

Josh Corner hesitated, his strong voice growing softer. "I've got to tell you Manny. I've not seen anything like this since we met on the *Ocean Duchess*. And maybe not even then."

Manny glanced at Chloe, then to Dean and Sophie.

"What does that mean, exactly?"

"It means Argyle had nothing up on this guy."

Shifting the phone to his other hand, Manny felt his stomach twist.

He'd prayed he would never see anything like what he'd seen on and off that ship at the hands of the Good Doctor. Friends who were like family had died horribly. It wasn't just the physical, but the mental games enjoyed by Argyle that caused him, and his unit, to lose sleep . . . still.

Josh hadn't said that exactly, but Manny could sense it.

He exhaled. "How do you know the killer's a man?"

"He left two rather pointed calling cards, according to the Miami-Dade Police Department detectives."

"Which are?"

Josh cleared his throat. "What he did to the bodies was probably enough to deduce the killer was male, but then he left something else."

"Again, what?"

"He left the set of knives he used to kill these poor people. He also carved his name into both of their chests and then onto their foreheads."

The rest of the air ran from Manny's lungs. "Name? Dammit. He gave a name and cut it twice into his victims?"

"Meet me in Florida. I'll have the Jet pick you up in the morning, six a.m. You'll have files showing what we and the Miami-Dade police have. Then you can meet Valentino."

CHAPTER-4

Kristen Luppo looked at the half-eaten chicken salad sandwich on her desk and sighed.

A good job in this economy, no matter how America's current set of politicians colored the employment market, was still hard to find. She'd taken this third shift position with the Miami-Dade Police Department's research division, hating the idea of working from ten p.m. to seven a.m. with a passion, but with the implied promise that as soon as something opened on either of the other shifts, that job was hers. That had been two years ago, and here she sat, eating crappy food, missing Miami's nightlife, and waiting hours, sometimes whole shifts, for something to do.

At least she was getting better at Words with Friends.

Her mom, Linda, had warned her to watch what comes out of people's mouths, that some people would say anything to get a job, but others would say anything to get her to take one.

"Cops, and mayors, can't be trusted," she'd said.

"Yeah, neither can men who say they love you," she whispered, answering her mother again.

She reached into her drawer, engaged in another quick look around the floor, not quite sure why. Only she and the damn mice knew she was there half of the time. She took a snort from her leather flask. Was there anything better than Caribbean rum?

She put the flask back in her drawer.

What choice did she have with this job anyway? She had to pay the bills, right? And, not to mention, she had to keep the wolves away from the door. God knew she had no sugar daddy to count on.

Dropping her feet to the floor, she rolled her chair closer to the twenty-two-inch computer monitor and caught her reflection. She ran a hand along her face, which was framed by her long auburn hair. She was still young and pretty enough to land a winner, a man who'd love her and take care of her. Maybe that wasn't every woman's dream, but to each his own. For her, a good man who'd take care of her would truly beat the hell out of this work arrangement.

Work? Hell, she wasn't even getting anything interesting to dive into and research these days, from the blues or the detectives. That in itself was a miracle and a curse. The night only moved slower with nothing to do. She found herself wishing for work, even though it would probably be of the ilk to curl her hair.

Miami was beautiful, with its gorgeous skyline, cruise ship ports, and never-ending social arenas, but it had its ugly, violent side. She'd seen a few crime scene photos that made her reload her flask a time or two.

Just when she was getting ready to email her friend, Millie, her email alert popped up telling her she had a request. A second later, the phone rang.

"Wow. Suddenly it's Grand Central Station around here," she said, picking up the receiver. "Research, this is Kristen."

She listened intently, felt her heart drop somewhere around her ankles, and then hung up the phone, her hand shaking.

Detective Duane James was an all-right guy, and not bad looking for being over sixty. Hey, he had most of his hair. But on the phone just now, she'd never heard him sound like that before. His voice was steady but not strong. He seemed . . . well, shaken. That in turn shook her, deeply.

His orders, however, had been explicit. She was to research all of the criminal databases available—international, federal, and local, including Interpol, VICAP, IAFIS, CODIS, and NCIC, for starters—for any mention, image, or wording that resembled the list he had just emailed her. And she was to get back to him pronto. He said the hotshots at the FBI's BAU were coming in, and this was part of their shtick.

He warned her it wasn't going to be easy to look at what he'd sent her, that the images were some of the very worst he'd ever witnessed, but that was how this cookie crumbled.

Cookie crumbled. She hadn't heard that term since she was a kid. She didn't like it now any more than she had then . . . because it meant there was no choice in the matter.

Reaching for her mouse, she inhaled, exhaled, inhaled, exhaled, and then opened the email from the detective. Attached were eleven photos and five documents. She typed in the password that would allow her access to them and clicked the first image.

Before she could stop it, she jerked her hand from the mouse and dove back into the sliding drawer again, this time taking a slug of rum that would make a sailor proud.

"Shit," she said.

Kristen started to replace the flask, shook her head, and took another deep draw. She knew she was going to need the artificial courage and then some.

She stared at the first image and then gathered courage enough to run her finger over the jagged word, not bothering to wipe the tears from her face.

Who could do this to someone, dead or alive? But that was why she wanted to become a cop. She wanted to help put away freaks like this forever.

Freak. The word certainly has taken on a completely new meaning with this . . . freak.

It took her fifteen minutes to finally open every attachment, and the images didn't get any easier to view. Once she had it all in front of her, her unique gift for spatial recognition and organizing took over.

She dragged the five documents to the top of her screen, using new interfacing software that allowed her to size them so that she could read a few lines at a time.

She took the pictures from the male victim first because it was obvious, even to a detective wannabe, that the perp had killed him first. Then she took the last five photos of the young woman's body and placed those directly below the man's.

After taking a few minutes to read the first document, she highlighted the words "Valentino" and "violent" then added "knives and cutting" and began the process of seeing if this bastard had raised his ugly head anywhere, anytime, in any state or any country before.

After about fifteen minutes of research, she realized she forgot to do something she always did this time of night. She pulled her cell phone from her blouse pocket and wrote a quick text to her mom. She told her good night and don't let the bed bugs bite. She hesitated and then told her she loved her.

A moment later, her mom gave her typical response, saying she wouldn't let anyone or anything in her bed except Kevin Costner, and then told Kristen she loved her too.

Going back to work, Kristen felt a little better. Mothers were the best protection against monsters, after all.

She was going to call on that protection tonight.

CHAPTER·5

The scent of Jen's hair reminded Manny of her mom, as did almost everything else about her. His daughter was a teenager only in years these days. She'd matured into the young woman he always imagined she would be, only tougher. Hell, she had to be tough or she might have ended up in some dark corner of a padded room, right beside him.

Maybe having to shoot a man had accelerated Jen's maturity; then again, maybe being able to make that decision had forced her to grow up, in an odd way.

Manny wondered what Louise would have thought of their baby girl. Really, he knew, though. Her puffed-out chest would have given her away.

Jen Williams released Manny and then hugged him again before holding him at arm's length.

"Be careful, Old Man, we've got Tiger tickets in a couple of weeks, you know."

"I know. I wouldn't miss it for the world. Besides, they cost me an arm and a leg."

"Yeah, I appreciate that. But where else can you see hot men dressed in tight white uniforms running around and bending over like that?"

He shook his head. Her mother's child indeed.

"You finish up your senior project, and we'll go over it when I get back."

She saluted smartly. "Aye, aye, *mon capitaine.*"

Pulling her hands into his, they stood face to face. "And, Jen. No matter what's going on, you can call me if you need to, right?"

Her eyes softened as she tilted her head and gave him a loving look. "I know, Dad, I know. I'm all right, though. I really am."

"Yep. You are, but don't forget to make me feel important, if you have the urge."

"Yeah, you old people need to feel wanted. Come on, dog."

One more hug, and she was off down the hallway toward her room with Sampson, their over-sized black lab and self-proclaimed protector of the realm.

Sampson stopped, looked back at Manny, and returned to rise up and lick his face, then rambled down the hall after Jen.

"Thanks for the kiss, Big Dog, I think," he said.

"She's a fine lass, Manny. She's as strong as they come, don't ya know."

Haley Rose, her green eyes as bright as he'd seen in weeks, leaned against the door casing between the kitchen and living room, stroking the ends of her red hair. The last month had taken a toll on her, and there were a few more stress lines around her eyes these days, but she was still a beautiful woman, even in her early fifties.

"She is, and thank God."

Stepping past his suitcase, he stood near his mother-in-law. "Almost as tough as her granny."

Smiling, Haley Rose touched Manny's face. "It's kind of ya to say so, Manny Williams. I just wish that toughness had not needed to be tested the way t'was."

"That's two of us, but we don't always get to make that call. And you three are here because of it."

She nodded. "True words ya say. Travel safely, and I promise ya some of my famous shepherd's pie when ya get home."

"Now, that's worth coming home for," he said with a wink.

Haley Rose pecked him on the cheek and then followed Jen's path to her own room. Her old swagger was on the way back, but it would take its time, he suspected.

"Boo!"

Turning in the other direction, he was met with a small round face inches from his own, thanks to his mother's outstretched hands. Ian possessed his mother's red hair, not his father's blond, but Ian had his dad's blue eyes. The combination was going to break a few hearts someday.

"Ohh. Got me," said Manny, jumping back.

Ian broke out in melodic laughter. The kind that melts any parent's heart and sticks with you hours later when you smile simply to think about it.

He took Ian from Chloe's arms, hugged him, and whispered how much he loved him . . . just before the tickle session broke loose.

After another round of laughing, he handed his son back to Chloe.

"Keep him revved up for me. Something tells me I'm going to need to hear that laugh."

"I think that's true, Manny Williams. That and a little close, personal contact from yer wife, I suspect." She reached up with one hand and pulled him to her soft lips.

Never, never would he tire of her kisses. Then there was the whole ever-present electrical charge that hailed from her touch. It had always been that way, and he prayed it would never stop.

The sensuality of her touch seemed to be magnified one hundred times over when they made love, like early this morning. She was able to awaken things in him that he feared had been lost when Louise had died.

The woman seemed born to bring out pleasure in him, and it made him want to find all of her switches as well. So far so good.

Their intimacy was more than that, however. Their time alone doubled as a sanctuary away from the worlds where they both lived, helping to balance the family world against the evil that would corrupt.

Chloe seemed to read his thoughts and reached down to squeeze his butt cheek. "I, too, have got a little promise or two to keep when you get home, man. We need more practice."

"Why yes you do. I'll be collecting too. Right after the shepherd's pie."

She ran her hand over his arm. "You'll have to figure out which one's hotter and better for you now, won't you?"

"No brainer," he said. "That shepherd's pie is to die for."

She hit him on the arm. "See how sleeping with pie does ya."

"Great point."

He kissed her and Ian again.

"You watch your back, Manny Williams. I love you, and I'll see you when you return."

He almost frowned. Almost gave away some of the dark thoughts, intuitions really, that he harbored regarding this case. He'd had some of those same feelings a time or two in the past when heading out to work a case. He supposed that was normal for cops who walked in the world where Manny and the BAU did.

In fact, it would probably indicate that something was wrong with him if he didn't feel a quota of paranoia or dread regarding his fate, and the fate of those who worked with him. They weren't exactly dealing with shoplifters and politicians.

He shook it off for the moment. There was more than one profiler in the Williams family, and he didn't want to incite more concern with Chloe.

"I can't wait," he said, smiling.

He kissed her full lips again and headed out the door, his scarred travel case in hand.

Usually Sophie would have picked him up, but Dean and his enigmatic friend had a couple of last minute errands to run and were going to meet him at the Capitol City Airport—with bows in her hair and a short mini skirt, she'd told him.

That made him smile as he climbed into the FBI's black SUV.

She just might do it.

Leaving the subdivision, he headed north, leaving his family behind once again. That was torture enough.

The thing he didn't leave behind was the sense of pending doom. As the darkness of the morning grew toward dawn, his feelings of apprehension grew more profound with each passing street light.

What the hell is wrong with you, Williams? You feel like a frightened school girl.

Maybe it was the whole thing with Chloe and Ian's attacker. That shitty incident had heightened his emotions, no question, and probably increased his sense of insecurity.

He sighed. "That's it, diagnose yourself and then prescribe the cure. Physician, heal thyself," he said out loud.

Back to focusing on the case. He'd have plenty of time for self-analysis later.

Flipping on the radio, the sudden blare of heavy metal guitars and unintelligible screaming caused his heart to skip a beat. He yanked the volume dial to the left, shaking his head.

Sophie.

She knew he didn't care for this type of music and certainly not at full volume.

She'd pranked him, again.

There had been the IcyHot gel in his underwear. Rubber snakes in his suitcase. And even shaving cream in his stocking cap last winter, among others. Not one time had he retaliated and dropped down to her level. Up until this minute, he thought acknowledging her little shenanigans would only encourage her and eventually she'd stop.

So much for that logic.

"Paybacks, Lee. It's time," he said.

Finding something far more to his liking, the smooth sounds of Boney James and his sax filled the SUV as he began his compartmental ritual. There could be few distractions on this case. He suspected they couldn't afford to miss a beat. Not one.

Manny turned west on 496 and slowly brought his concentration toward the Miami killer and his heinous actions. He'd not seen the crime scene photos yet, so he did an inventory on what he knew about killers who named themselves.

They were ultra-organized, leaving little to chance regarding the possibility of being caught, which demonstrated a fallacy regarding the theory that most serial killers *wanted* to be captured. Spending the rest of their lives in prison or getting a lethal injection or a hot chair wasn't on serial killers' agendas, ever.

Killers like this one usually stalked their victims, took them to a second location for the kill, and, most times, found a third location to dispose of the bodies in an effort to confuse the police further. Three potential crime scenes were far more difficult to locate and forensically process than one.

This killer hadn't gone to step three, however. He'd killed and left the victims in the same area. And, according to Josh, had seemingly brought and left behind his own knives.

Manny scowled, his stomach doing one of those fluttery circles. It wasn't typical to leave the bodies where Valentino had, but to abandon his killing instrument of choice . . . that was almost unheard of. In fact, Manny couldn't recall running across that situation before, and he'd been doing this for years. Dahmer had been caught with his saws and knives in his apartment, but he hadn't left them on display for the Milwaukee police to find.

Valentino leaving his weapons was a dangerous move. In this day and age of forensic science and procedures, that act alone could get him caught. So, why? Manny would normally think of it as a throw-it-in-your-face kind of thing, but he wasn't sure, at least until he had more information. Still, it didn't *feel* right.

Reaching the airport, Manny drove into long-term parking and turned off the engine.

Valentino was arrogant and confident, no question about that. The act of naming himself was clearly a narcissistic move.

Getting out of the vehicle, he grabbed the roll of antacids from the dash—he was going to need them—and headed for the tarmac and the FBI's Gulf Stream V.

He shifted his travel bag to the other hand, his mind racing.

There was at least one more thing he knew about serial killers who named themselves, as rare as that act was. Usually it was the press who did that sort of thing, believing themselves to be clever.

Killers like Valentino didn't stop until they were caught. If they were caught at all.

CHAPTER-6

"Hey, Williams, how did you like that music? I couldn't turn it up any louder, but you know, those SUVs have great sound systems."

Entering the jet, Manny acted as if he hadn't heard Sophie. He opened the portside closet, put his bag inside, and then headed for the seat facing her.

"Williams? Are you listening? Did you hear my ass?"

He continued to ignore her, careful not to look at her face as he played with the seatbelt.

She reached over and touched his arm, a trace of frustration now creeping into her voice and body language.

Feigning to be startled, he put his hand to his chest as he stared at her, then looked relieved as if first noticing Sophie.

"Sorry. I can't hear anything. Someone left the radio on full-bore in my truck, and I've not been able to hear much since then. I went to the emergency room, and the doctor thinks I might have a condition called NIHL. Noise-induced hearing loss."

Sophie's frustration morphed into a guarded concern.

"Bullshit, Williams. That can't happen."

"What? Say that again, slower. I have to read your lips."

"I. Said. Bullshit. That. Can't Happen," she repeated, becoming louder and slower in her speech pattern as her alarm grew.

"I said that too," he said, getting louder himself. "But apparently I had a preexisting condition, and all of the flying and gun training and whatever has weakened my ear structure. He said that it happens and people don't even know it, then bam, some one-time loud noise could deafen someone. Maybe for good."

Dean leaned forward from his seat beside Sophie, stroking his beard, his dark eyes alive. "I've heard of that. I actually had a case in LA that revolved around that same thing. If noise grows above eighty-five decibels, it can begin to affect our hearing. If it gets to, like, one-twenty to, like, one-fifty, people with a weakened hearing system can lose their hearing in one or both ears."

Even though there remained a tiny thread of doubt on Sophie's face, having her husband corroborate Manny's story seemed to be driving her closer to the edge of belief.

"Are you kidding? How come I've never heard of that?" she asked, her voice even louder.

Manny shouted back, "I hadn't either, but it's real. I just wish I knew who screwed up and left the music up so loud."

He watched her eyes dart back and forth. He knew her wheels were turning and could guess what was coming next.

Confession was always good for the soul.

She got out of her seat and turned away from him, speaking softly in an obvious attempt to get him to trip up. "I think you're jerking my chain. You know I turned that music up, don't you?"

Manny glanced at Dean and shrugged his shoulders. "Did she say something?"

"I think so, but I didn't quite catch it. Watch my lips closely. Are you really still going to Miami?"

Manny answered with all of the slow speech and high volume he could muster. "Yes. I'm still going. The doc said the flight won't bother me, but if my hearing doesn't come back in a few days, I'm to come home immediately. They might have to do some surgical procedure to restore at least some of my hearing."

Manny waited, embracing the pregnant silence and enjoying the sweat, literal and figurative, that his partner was boiling in.

It didn't take long.

Sophie spun around, grabbed Manny's face with both hands, true anguish on her face, her eyes glistening. "This is my fault. I'm sorry. It was just a prank. I didn't mean to cause this. Damn it. I was just playing around."

"Cause what? What the hell did you do this time, Lee?"

Manny freed himself from Sophie's grip and turned to see Josh Corner entering the jet with Belle Simmons right behind him.

"Hey, Josh. Good to see you two. Oh, she was dinking around again, and I thought it time to reverse the tables and enjoy a little payback, teach her a lesson."

Sophie stood up straight, her hands on her hips, moving from remorse to pissy in two seconds flat. Her eyes began twitching as she looked from Manny to Dean, then to Josh and Belle. Then back to Manny and Dean.

"I'm not sure which one of you to kill first. Or how. But it's going to hurt like hell. I'm going to make it last for days. And I'm going to do it wearing leather and using a whip."

"Oh, that's far too much information for me, Sophie," said Manny, laughing.

"That wasn't for you, big boy that was for my loving husband. I want him to see what he can't touch, ever again. All the while, I'll be pulling his beard out one hair at a time. Maybe his pubes too."

"Ouch," said Josh.

Bending back down to within an inch of Manny's face, squeezing again. "As for you,

Guardian of the Universe. I'm going to ... to remember that one. That was pretty good, once I got over the shock. You got me, boy. But—"

"But what? You can't stand not having the last laugh so I need to watch my ass, right?"

"Yep. You're even smarter than I thought, for a blond, blue-eyed, over-forty cop who should be looking at rocking chairs instead of chasing serial killers and shit."

"I don't think you should keep your feelings inside. I think you should let them out," said Manny, straight faced.

"Funny."

She kissed him on the forehead. "Just know mama's coming for you, and it won't be pretty."

"I bet it won't. I can't wait to see what's next. But right now we have to get our fannies in motion." said Josh, his cobalt blue eyes bright.

Manny rose from his chair and shook Josh's hand. "Great to see you."

"You too."

He then gave Belle a hug and stepped back. "You ready for this one? It's not like we're on Cozumel or anything."

Belle's laugh was genuine, adding to the setting of the jet's cabin.

"True enough, Manny. Now that I've gotten my feet wet, I can't wait to help bring this one down."

The frown came and went from her pretty face, causing Manny's mood to darken some. Belle was a talented profiler who had seen a few things, especially in light of her work as a forensic tech and detective in DC. Her sudden change in mood indicated to him that she was already feeling the weight of the case.

"So you've seen the crime scene reports and photos?" he asked.

"Sort of. Josh wanted to wait until we could all look at them together. I respect that. But I just had to take a quick trip through both files on the way up here this morning to see if I could pick up anything right off the bat."

"I get that. I couldn't have waited for an hour and half flight either. So, did you see anything?"

"Yes, I did. I made a couple of notes, but that's for later," she said.

"I'm looking forward to hearing what you saw."

"Yeah, let's do that when we get airborne, my favorite part of this job," said Sophie. She then hugged Josh and Belle, Dean following right behind her, making the reuniting of the BAU complete.

While watching the group's interaction with each other, Manny was struck with how much they leaned on each other. Not simply in the professional sense, although that was true, but in the emotional arena. What they did, what they saw collectively, reflected the bizarre of the bizarre, the darkest reaches of the human condition. Their job consequently showed them places most humans need not see, not even on the boob tube.

God knew, at times, they all needed a hand to pull them out of those terrible places. He couldn't think of anyone better to make that happen than these people.

He was grateful for that.

A minute later, the pilot came out of the cockpit and told them they had five minutes until take off and would be in the air for about two hours, putting them in Miami at around eight thirty a.m.

"Okay, thanks. Time to buckle up," said Josh.

Twenty minutes later, they were over Detroit when Josh called them together.

His boss and friend was a good cop, but Josh's real gift was getting things organized, which recently had included his personal life. He carried himself a bit differently these days, and Manny was glad for the confidence he showed. A strong family life can do that for folks.

"Let's gather at the table. We've actually got three files to analyze. One file from Miami-Dade police, one from their forensics division, and one from our folks in Quantico. That one is a bit thin because of time constraints, but there are some items of interest in there."

They moved to the small conference table, Sophie doing quite well despite her hatred of flying and her propensity toward motion sickness. She was only a bit pale this time.

"You all right, Sophie?" he asked.

"Yeah, yeah. I took some nausea stuff before we left and feel pretty good. It's not as good as tequila, but it does the trick."

"That would have disappointed Alex," said Josh.

"Yeah, well, he'll have to get his jollies another way."

"Okay, now that we have the medical report out of the way, let's get to work," said Josh.

"Bite me, Corner. I'd rather be taking a train, you know."

He laughed. "I know. I appreciate your valor."

"You bet your ass you do."

"Me too," said Dean.

"Are you sucking up? It ain't going to work. Helping Williams gag me wasn't that funny. It'll be so cold on my side of the bed you're going to think you're a celibate Tibetan monk before this is over."

"Yes, my queen," he answered.

"That's better."

She touched his hand without looking at him.

True love was different for every couple, no question, but there were not many loves like the one Dean and Sophie carried. *Until death do you part* held true meaning for them.

"Okay. The first file is the actual crime scene reports and has most of the important photos from the first team who arrived at the site. The second team from their CSU hadn't finished their report when I received the call."

"I know this is one of those murders from hell, but isn't it unusual to call us after one incident?" asked Belle.

"It is," said Josh. "But the senior detective in charge, an old friend of ours, Marie Swifton, insisted we be invited in right away. We'd worked with her a couple of years ago involving *Carousel Cruise Line* employees. She told me she thought she knew where this was headed."

"So they want a profile pronto?" asked Dean.

"They do. So let's get to work. You have thirty minutes to go over these files and then talk about what you see here, as usual," said Josh.

Manny embraced the silence and began doing what he was born to do, like it or not, and that was to profile killers who'd left their terrible mark on society and the unfortunate victims.

He opened the crime scene file containing the photos and began studying them—one at a time, slowly. Then he repeated the process, which was his custom in such cases.

On the outside, he appeared calm, collected, professional, and objective. Looking only for facts and hidden clues. But that calm demeanor hid the cornucopia of emotions and startling impressions that now rattled around in his head, waging war against every sense of decency and compassion.

These images of revulsion were exactly that. These two had been alive, the Welch couple, and just married before this butcher stole their futures. Was there a more blatant sin than to steal someone's future?

Compartmentalizing his emotions and magnifying his concentration allowed him to notice practically everything.

The images clearly showed how the counterclockwise circles, displayed by the folds on the skin, connected and cut into the skin of both victims, the varying degrees of depth, the amount of blood on and around the victims. The specific source of that blood. The bindings the killer had used and the extent the ligature marks had damaged the arms, the neck, and the ankles.

He made mental notes of the size of the tree and the northerly direction the killer had stood as he faced the man and then the westerly side of the tree for the woman. Significant? Maybe.

What of the build and body types of each of the victims? The color of their hair and eyes? The size of their feet? The tanned pigment of their skin? What they did for a living? Did all of that play a part? Or did none of it?

He wasn't sure, but he was beginning to get a feel for this one, at least a tiny version of intent as the collage began to melt into a defined portrait.

Manny took out his customized Swiss Army knife and unfolded the nail file. He then began to trace the precisely carved "VALENTINO" on the man's face and then his chest. He repeated the act with the photos of the woman. In each case, the meticulous connected circles on each body and lettering had been perfect. Detailed right down to a small curl on the tail of each "N."

Running his hand through his hair, he examined the photos a third time, and then closed the file without reading the reports. Nor did he open and read the other two files. He didn't need to see what was in them.

Instead, he got up and went to the jet's Keurig machine and brewed a cup of hazelnut crème. The aroma of the coffee was almost as satisfying as the coffee itself.

"That coffee smells damn good Williams. Are you getting me a cup too?" asked Sophie, shutting the last of the three files.

Manny returned to the table with his cup in hand. "I don't think you should add more caffeine into your system, your middle name is wired."

"Real cute. I'll get my own. And you're supposed to be a gentleman."

"I'll get you a cup," said Dean. "After the shit in those files, I just may spike yours and mine with the good old-fashioned whiskey of our choice."

"I hear you," said Belle, rising out of her chair.

"That'll be an 'all for one and one for all' decision," said Josh. "I think I'll be in need of both as well."

Five minutes later, they'd reassembled. Manny guessed his talented crew was ready to tackle what they'd seen. He knew he was.

Josh began. "Before we start brainstorming here, I want to let you know something else. After the call from the Miami folks, Manny and I talked some more and decided we also wanted them to research cold cases, nationwide and internationally, that might have anything similar in terms of MO. We thought, or at least Manny did, that there might be a case or two in the past that could possibly be related to this one."

"You don't think this is his first rodeo," said Sophie.

"You all know the typical profiles on these killers. Especially given the organized vein this double murder seems to be," said Manny.

"You mean the whole 'let's practice our trade on a surrogate target'?" asked Belle, leaning in over the small metal table, her eyes shining.

Listening to her verbalize his words gave Manny pause.

Over and over, the remarks she'd made regarding serial killers proved to be true, especially in regard to particularly pointed, merciless killers who had developed their "trade" as a horrific form of psychological evolution.

And, invariably, the eventual target of their hatred would become a victim. Often the last one because they'd actually worked up enough courage to confront their personal tormentor and rid themselves of that tormentor.

"Yes, I think so, Belle. Ed Kemper, the Co-ed Killer who murdered and dismembered six young women in the Santa Cruz area, comes to mind," Manny said. "After his compulsion caused him to kill his grandparents at age fifteen, he claims his desire to see what it was like to kill led to the other murders. He then, after killing five of the six co-eds, butchered his mother by decapitating her and tearing out her vocal cords, which he then put in the garbage disposal. He killed her best friend a few minutes later. After a quick trip though a few states out west, he called the police to turn himself in. He said he was done killing," said Manny.

"Damn. Talk about hating your mother. That was the big dude, right?" asked Sophie.

"His file says he was six-nine and about three hundred pounds, and as an added kicker, to show what the cops and his victims had been up against, his IQ was way over one hundred forty," said Josh.

"Those poor girls never had a chance," said Belle softly.

She swiveled her chair toward Manny. There was that brief frown again. "Okay, that was an extreme case, but it fits the profile, and I can understand why you'd want to check cold cases, but tell me how that ties in with this one."

"Yeah, you haven't even looked at the other two files," said Dean. "And yes, I noticed."

"Good questions. But before I answer that, let's talk about our own FBI rules that help us to define a true serial killer."

"Okay, I'll bite," said Sophie. "They kill more than three folks with a cooling-off period in between. From the looks of things, that doesn't apply, yet."

"Right, maybe," said Manny.

"We don't know if he knew the victims, but probably didn't," said Josh.

"Right again. 'Probably' being the operative word."

"It looks like he had a need to dominate the victims violently and sadistically. Mission accomplished there," said Belle.

"I don't think he did this for the money," said Josh. "And one murder I can buy as a symbolic death for what or who was getting into his craw. It seems like overkill to assume that he hated two people to the same degree. Not even a set of parents."

"I think that's a fair assessment, Josh. Almost always the reason for killing with these folks is a singular purpose or thought, although collateral damage isn't unheard of," said Manny.

"True. But he took the time to mark them the same way with those connecting circles and he disemboweled the woman as well as the man. That reeks of equal treatment, right?" said Belle.

"Hallelujah. Women are now equal with men, at least in this prick's world," said Sophie through her teeth.

"Now if we can just get equal pay," said Belle.

"Yeah. How much do you make, Williams?" asked Sophie.

"Really? Now?" said Manny.

"Okay. Your tight butt is off the hook for now, but you owe me an answer later."

"What's the last rule we use to define a serial killer?" asked Manny.

"The victims are typically vulnerable, like prostitutes or runaways or homeless. They all make easy targets and people won't know they're missing, maybe even for months or years," said Josh.

"This couple most certainly didn't fit that category. Both had most of their families living in South Florida. They both graduated from Miami University and both had good-paying jobs. They were also socially active, according to one interview in the file," said Belle, then glanced at Manny. "You knew that, though, without even looking at the file from our folks in Quantico."

"I had a hunch. These two had no signs that indicated one was the victim and the other collateral damage. They most certainly appeared to be healthy, sun-loving people. Not overweight or too thin. Probably some people even considered them vain and a tad snotty," answered Manny. "That doesn't translate to an easy target."

The only sound filtering though the impromptu silence was the dull whine of the jet boring through the air at thirty-five thousand feet as his unit reflected on the last few minutes of conversation. He wanted someone to speak, to see what he'd seen. To express what he already knew was true.

Manny waited.

Finally Belle broke the silence. "These murders are a hodge-podge of hits and misses. They don't fit a true profile of a typical serial killer, but in some areas they do, right?"

Manny nodded. "I don't think this killer is typical anything."

"What does that mean?" asked Sophie.

Exhaling, Manny leaned over the table just as they hit a tiny air pocket. The jet dropped a few feet and then steadied itself.

Sophie yelped, the momentary look on her face displaying pure terror. She recovered quickly, hand still on her chest, and scanned his face. "Good God, that sucks. I think my guts are in my throat. Anyway, explain yourself, son."

"I hope I can. It sounds strange to say, but I think this murderer's only motivation is the pure joy of killing."

CHAPTER-7

The soft light emanating from her computer tower served as a night light, and she welcomed it. Not in the true sense that it brought her protection from the hideous demons and monsters, stinking of sulfur and dealing in death, that might crawl out from underneath her bed or burst from the closet and tear her to shreds. She held no such fears, at least for now. There was a time, those years ago when she pondered such supernatural possibilities, and God knew she had reason, but not now. That time was over.

The steady blue light allowed her to see clearly. It's rhythm a reflection of her own internal war. And war it was.

All of her life she'd been taught, and had passed it on as well, that we must be about good things, however such a nebulous word can be defined.

Watch your manners. Be polite. Be respectful. Dress correctly. Don't smoke; don't overdrink;

don't spread your legs for anyone but the man who would be your husband. Think of others as more important than yourself. Don't lie. Don't swear. Don't cheat on your taxes, and God forbid you were contrary to your parents and spoke in a manner of boldness. That particular violation of the Ten Commandments was a one-way ticket to hell from which there was no return.

But none of that applied to her anymore. Especially not since the incident.

She'd paid her dues up to that point and, for the most part, had tolerated the game of life and its unpredictable expectations. And, at certain times over the years, had even enjoyed it.

She rolled over on her back and stared at the ceiling.

The incident.

Is that how she was identifying it now?

Calling that state of affairs an incident, she supposed, was far easier than calling it by its proper name.

The memories had been masked, at least mostly, but forever was a long time. Most days, it worked.

Yet, she never really could get the girl out of her mind, and the dark thoughts that accompanied her. No matter how desperately she tried, that face was always at the forefront of her mind, taunting her under the guise of being a loving, caring person. The girl had even told her she loved her.

"My ass," she whispered.

She knew the real truth. She knew the motivation possessed by the little slut who'd ruined everything for her and denied her true happiness. That's all she really wanted, to be happy. No one had the right to deny that to another, no one.

She clenched the comforter in her hands, nails digging into her palms even through the blanket.

That bitch had said she did it to protect her from pain. Bullshit. What did that slut know about pain? She lived a perfect little life right up until that day and even beyond.

But that was going to change.

Her tormentor had taken away the only real happiness she'd experienced in this screwed up life, and payment was due.

"An eye for an eye," she said softly. "An eye for an eye."

Then, content in her mission and knowing what had to happen next, she rolled over and fell fast asleep.

CHAPTER-8

"How are you doing this morning, mother? The sun is going to be a bright one. I brought you some of those Whoppers that you like," he said.

The woman sitting in the rocker facing the windows of the lanai turned her head slowly and smiled at her son. "I love those things. Thank you, Peter. You made an old lady's day, you know."

Striding to her right side, he sat in the matching oak rocker.

"Old? Oh, you're not old at all. You're kind of like one of those cougar women. If I weren't your son, I'd be after you for myself. You're still very beautiful."

She laughed, placing a thin, feeble hand on his arm. "Thank you, even though I know you're lying like the rug under my feet. It's still nice to hear. You were always such a good boy, and now you're even a better man."

"Ohh, I bet you say that to all of your kids."

"I do, silly. You know you're my only child though, so don't mess with your old mother."

Peter leaned back in the chair and began a slow, rhythmic motion. "I don't really mess with you. I just like to see that smile come shining through. It makes me feel better."

"I know. It makes me feel better as well."

She coughed, then coughed again louder, then a third time, worse than the first two. He shot out of his chair and was down on one knee in front of her.

After one more chest-wrenching cough that he thought would produce a lung on the lanai's floor, she stopped, both hands on her thin chest. She raised her head, eyes moist, the absent color returning to her face. She smiled weakly. "That hurt a little, but I'll live."

"Thank God. I hate those fits," he said.

"No more than I, son. But you need to listen to me. I'll live today, but I don't have much time, and we both know that. I'm eighty-eight, and the cancer is getting worse."

"Mom, can we not—"

"No. We will talk about this. I'm checking out soon. I've had a great life, but there is one thing I want to see."

She looked at him, her fading blue eyes almost matching her gray mane.

He waited for her to continue as she cleared her throat, as if he didn't know where this was heading.

"I am a bit worried that you have no one to take care of you, to watch over you. No grandchildren to carry on our family name and our heritage. I know that's an old-fashioned, romantic thought these days, but it's true. Especially the part of having someone to take care of you, to have someone to grow old with. There are so many young ladies in Miami that would die to have a man like you. You know, good looking and loaded."

It was his turn to smile. "Good looking and loaded, huh? You're still a charmer. Okay. Okay. I know, Mom, we've talked of this several times. I'll take care of what I want in my life when the time comes. It's just not a priority right now. You and my business are all that I care for and really have time to be committed to. Dating can be a complication for a forty-five-year-old workaholic who thinks his mother is the most important woman on the planet."

"So, you'll promise me that you will find the right woman when I'm gone, right?"

Peter looked at the veins on the back of his hands. He hated promises because he hated lying in general. Most promises ended up as lies, in his estimation, but what could he say?

"I will. When the time is right, I will, okay? Happy?"

"Yes. I am. And you'll thank me," she answered, a twinkle in her eyes.

A bird began chirping, and Peter realized it was his mother's customized doorbell.

"I'll get it."

Peter rose from his knee and walked through the house to the front door. He pulled the mahogany door open and scanned the average-looking man dressed in a blue delivery company uniform that he vaguely recognized. The man held a package under one arm and a clipboard in the other.

"Can I help you?"

"Yes sir. Is this the home of Gladys Blanks?"

"Yes, it is."

"I have a delivery."

"Really? I didn't know my mother ordered anything. That's not like her."

The man shrugged, his cap rising a little higher on his forehead. He was still squinting in the early morning sun. "I just deliver them pal. I need a signature."

Peter sighed. What was this world coming to? People getting rid of their landlines because their only phone calls were from telemarketers. There were countless charities constantly begging for money, looking to take advantage of the old, weak, and ignorant. Now his mother was getting a package that he'd bet a thousand dollars she hadn't ordered.

"Who is it from?"

The delivery man glanced at the address label, the beginnings of impatience showing in his expression. "It says it's from Miami City Cemetery. Does that mean anything to you?"

It did. The city's cemetery was where his father had been buried six years ago, and it would be where his mother and he would spend eternity, at least in the physical sense.

Peter was swamped with a sudden sense of nostalgia. He remembered the day, the hour, that he and his parents had bought the plots and paid for the headstones some ten years ago. It had been a melancholy day, but then later, they'd gone to South Beach and eaten at Joe's Stone Crab.

After a wonderful meal, they had driven past the cruise ships in port, something his parents loved to see.

"Sir?"

"Yes. I'm sorry, just walking down memory lane."

He opened the door and motioned for the man to step inside.

"Where do I sign? I don't know what this is, but it might be an omen, you know?"

"I do know." The delivery man pulled out the Taser from his pocket and forced it into Peter's chest.

Peter dropped to his knees, his body pulsing like he was in a massage chair going a hundred miles per hour.

"Wh-what are—?"

He was hit again, this time in the back of the neck. He fell to the floor, intense pain coursing throughout his body. On top of that, he was unable to move. A second later, he felt his bladder give way and could do nothing to stop it.

The delivery man stooped over his stricken body, a confident grin on his face, the stench of onions on his breath.

"I want to thank you for letting me in, Peter. I've been watching you and your mother for a while now and, I must say, you are a dedicated son. But I wonder, does she know about your other life? I'd bet not. Don't worry. I won't tell her. Well, at least not until the very end."

He tried to shake his head, to speak, to tell the man to leave his mother alone, and to not destroy her hope for him.

Another jolt raced through his body as this crazy bastard Tased him again, this time in the thigh, ending any more coherent thought.

He saw the darkness awaiting him on the fringe of his vision and fought it, fought like hell. Then just as his mind began to clear, one more jolt ended his struggle as it ushered in the bliss of a painless dark.

The last thing he thought of was his mother, sweet Gladys who never harmed anyone, and how she'd cope with whatever hell was coming next.

CHAPTER-9

The sun peeked through the port window of the jet as Manny finished his coffee.

He knew he'd surprised his staff and perhaps himself with his declaration, but it was what it was. This lunatic was different from the others, far different.

Argyle had a twisted, vengeful purpose and a God complex.

Anna Ruiz said she'd been sorting things out and then had a revelation.

Caleb Corner had proclaimed himself protector of the rain forest in Puerto Rico.

Mike Crosby had simply snapped and acted out his life-long hatred of cops, and apparently Manny. His anger had manifested itself after his new bride, Lexi, had been killed.

There had been other killers over the last few years who'd exhibited classic behavior, at least for the most part. Each had a subtle, specialized beat that he or she followed. Still, they could all eventually be categorized, their styles analyzed enough to lead to a predicted behavior. They'd each had a trigger event in their lives, and that was always somewhere to start and eventually end an investigation.

Manny wasn't sure that was true about this one.

"What the hell does that mean? All of these pricks have a reason to kill, and I've never heard of any of them doing it just for the fun of it," said Dean, his face tight.

"I have to agree with Dean on that, Williams," said Sophie.

"First, just realize that this is my best guess, okay?"

"We usually like your guesses, though," said Josh.

Manny glanced at Belle to await her response, and he got none. Instead, she was exploring his face, almost begging him to continue. There was apprehension in her expression as well.

"What is it, Belle?"

"Well, it just has to do with a note I wrote on the side of one of the pictures when I went through the Dade County photos the first time."

"And?"

"I wrote that he likes what he does, that's all."

"Why do you think you wrote that? Did it have anything to do with the time between the Welch's deaths?"

"Yes, for one thing. It looks like they died maybe three hours apart, if the ME's timeline is correct. That means he took his sweet time getting to the woman after taking out her husband."

It was *his* turn to examine *her* face.

"What's the other?"

"We've seen these killers be meticulous in uncanny ways, yet, this one . . . his care seems over the top, even for these types of killers," she said, glancing down to the table, obviously uncomfortable.

He understood that part. It had taken a few cases for him to say what was on his mind in front of the other detectives when he first started meeting with a new group of people. No one wanted to think the new person had a crazy side.

Was that all, though?

Her mannerisms indicated she was past nervous and maybe even a little fearful. It was probably nothing, and he'd been wrong before. Still, they'd talk later, in private, just to make sure.

"Good thoughts and insight, Belle. Part of what you said makes me feel like this trip could be a different one for the BAU," said Manny.

There it was again. That sense of dread and impending doom. Maybe he needed to use some of those happy pills when he got home because his paranoia was getting a workout.

"Well, don't be shy cowboy, get to it," said Sophie.

Before Manny could respond, the pilot came over the intercom and said they had about forty-five minutes until they were on the ground.

"Do they have to say it that way?" asked Josh, angst peeking from his face.

The memory of his and Chloe's nearly fatal crash in Youngstown rose up into Manny's mind. He suspected the memory of that event was the reason for Josh's comment and momentary anxiety.

"I thought you were over that whole plane crash episode," said Manny.

"Over it and thinking about it are two different things," said Josh.

"Pansy-ass," said Sophie, grinning.

"Oh, that's coming from Miss Puke-my-guts-out every time we take off and land. You would have died of a heart attack, right after you messed yourself," said Josh.

"Yeah, good point. But I would have done it in style."

"Plane crash? What plane crash?" asked Belle.

"I'll tell you later. Let's stay on track, Manny," said Josh.

"Oh, I can't wait for that one," said Belle.

"It'll be a pisser of a story and, of course, he comes out a hero. Rumor is that Chloe saved his ass, though," said Sophie.

"I plead the fifth on everything," said Josh.

"Figures. Oh, wait a second. I have to make a call."

She pulled her phone from her pocket and hit a speed-dial button.

"We don't have a lot of time. What are you doing?" asked Josh.

She raised a finger in the classic hold-on gesture.

"Hey, Dough Boy, I just wanted to call and tell you that we'll be fine. Belle's really smart so you can take all of the time you need. Hell, maybe they'll even let you go, you know, fire your ass. And no doughnuts before surgery."

She hesitated, listening to Alex's response, an impish expression radiating from her brown eyes.

"That wasn't very nice. I don't think that's humanly possible for me anyway, but I'll talk to Dean about the science of doing one's self."

Another pause, then she answered again.

"I'm pretty sure that's not going to happen either, but you paint a vivid picture. Take care. We'll be thinking of you, sort of."

She hung up, put the phone away, folded her hands together, and sat still, a content look on her face.

"Was that necessary?" asked Manny.

"Hell yeah. He's got to know that we care. He'll be heading into surgery in a while, so I had to lift his spirits."

"Care? You called Alex names and told him he was going to lose his job," said Josh, shaking his head.

"I did. That's what friends are for. Besides, he got his two cents worth too, and I think it made him feel better."

"What did he tell you to do?" asked Dean.

"Oh, I'm a lady. I don't talk that way. That's between him and me anyway," she said.

"I don't get you two, but are we done with this stuff? We have murders to solve," said Josh.

"Yep, I'm done. Go ahead, Manny. I've got a couple notes and questions myself," answered Sophie.

Love wore different clothes for most of us, but he doubted that the wardrobe could be more bizarre for Sophie and Alex. And make no mistake, they loved each other like the closest of brothers and sisters.

He shifted in his seat and began.

"Like Belle said, these murders took an inordinate amount of time. Torture can last awhile in these situations, and this was definitely torture, but I don't think the killer looks at it that way at all."

"Why?" asked Josh.

"Time is always an issue for unsubs like this one. They like the torture aspect, which almost always possesses a sexual component, which doesn't appear to be the case here, yet they don't want to get caught either. No matter how comfortable they are with the setting when the murders begin, their paranoid minds get the best of them."

"So near the end of the ordeal, after they've played out their perverted fantasies, they speed things up because they become nervous and a little impatient that someone will see them. That leads to sloppy behavior, or at least less precise actions than when they began their ritual. I don't see that here."

"You know that how?" asked Sophie.

"You're talking about the precision in the carving of 'Valentino' on the victim's bodies, right? I mean, the monograms on the woman are just as perfect as the ones on the man, who he probably killed a full three hours sooner," said Belle.

"Right. That proves to me he wasn't in a hurry. He had complete confidence in his plan and knew he wouldn't be disturbed in his location. That, or his enjoyment was far more important than any other concern, like getting caught," said Manny.

"If he's as organized as we think, then we have to go with well-planned and not worried about being discovered," said Sophie.

"I think so. Yet, spending a minimum of four to six hours outside, even at night, engaging in this sort of activity is risky," said Manny.

"Unless he *knew* there was no issue with it," said Josh.

"I'm sure the locals are checking out how often the land was patrolled and when," said Dean.

"I would, but what if the risk was part of the high? You know, the adrenaline rush," said Belle.

"That's possible. Yet, at least now, he doesn't seem like a risk taker to me. I think he has total control over his emotions and kept his focus before he indulged in his—"

Manny stopped.

His what? His fantasy? No, he didn't think so. They already knew, according to the preliminary report, that these murders weren't driven by anything sexual.

Revenge? There was nothing indicating anger-driven actions even though he killed them savagely. He didn't mutilate the victims in a conventional way. Nor had he embarrassed them by making them look like something less than human, in Manny's way of thinking.

The devil was in the details.

"I know that look. What, Williams? What were you going to say?" said Sophie.

"I don't know for sure. I was just struck with this whole picture of preciseness for both victims. Like he was performing his job with great pride. Maybe he believes it's his vocation, his calling. Even his destiny. No revenge. No Anger. No fantasy. Just killing and doing it precisely, efficiently, and with great attention to detail."

"We've seen detail before, though. Like that sick bitch in Houston last fall," said Sophie.

"True, but that was anger related, as we found out later. He hated his abusive sister and everyone who looked like her. And, if you recall, he got sloppy with the last two victims. That's how we caught him," said Manny.

"Oh yeah, right. But you left my Asian ass in Chicago for a couple of days, remember? And I didn't get to see everything first hand."

"Hey, thank God for little favors," said Dean.

"Well, that's true. I hate giving the dark side more nightmare fodder."

"Don't we all. What else makes you think that way, Manny?" asked Josh.

"I know leaving your tools behind isn't a way to go about your business, but he left his knives."

"How would that work in his thinking? That part looks like, to me, that he is stuffing it in law enforcement's face," said Josh.

"It does on the surface. But it isn't, in my mind. I think he's done with those knives. I think he believes that they've done their job and he doesn't need those tools anymore."

"Like being finished with a broken pencil or an empty pen?" asked Belle.

"Yes. Good analogy. But I'd take it a step further. He doesn't need this special set of tools any longer. I think it's more like using a football to begin a baseball game. Or an artist who is finished with a particular set of brushes and wants or needs different ones to get the right effect."

"We've run into some of these types of killers who thought they were expressing their art, or wanted us to believe that. Josh's stepbrother Caleb for one, but this goes far deeper."

"I know, and he may have some of that thought process, but I think it's far different than that."

God in heaven, why did he see so clearly into the minds of creeps like this? These insights were enough to drive most any man insane. After reorganizing his thoughts, he exhaled before he answered. "I don't believe he thinks these blades will work for what he has coming next."

Manny felt the chill himself as the statement escaped his mouth.

He didn't look around the silent circle to verify what he already knew because his unit realized the truth of those words almost as deeply as he did.

A few minutes later, the jet settled into its final descent and then landed lightly on the tarmac.

As they rolled to a stop, Sophie softly broke the silence.

"Shit. What *is* next, Manny?"

"I'm afraid we're going to find out," he answered.

CHAPTER-10

Libby Cossaboom sighed in the direction of her husband.

"Come on, John. I told Gladys we'd take her to the mall; and we're already late."

John brushed his silver hair back from his forehead, but refused to pick up the pace. He was retired, by God.

The love of his life was still that and more, but at age seventy-eight, he wasn't hurrying for anyone anymore. It was bad enough he had to cancel his Monday morning round of golf with his friends, but then to have to go shopping with two old women under the guise of watching out for them . . . well, that just took the balls right out of his sac, what was left of them.

The boys understood because they had wives too. They always understood, but that wouldn't stop the bantering the next week, especially from Manis and Prisby, about his seemingly pussy-whipped condition, as they would put it. Eberle would take it a step further; he'd go the whole round meowing like some damned horny tomcat.

John would be lining up a six-footer and somewhere out of the background would come the soft "meeooww, meeooww."

He would just shake his head and sink the putt anyway, take their money. He smiled at that. There was nothing like taking the money of good friends who had mocked you all morning.

None of that was the point, not truly, however. He'd miss time with his friends, and God knew none of them had much of that precious commodity left. But when it came to the slim woman he'd married those many years ago, everyone else was second. Conversely, it didn't mean he had to like going to the mall either.

"John. We only have to walk two blocks, c'mon."

"Libby, for the last time, you're just lucky I'm driving you to the mall, okay?"

She stopped, turned around, stepped back to him, and took both of his hands. "I know. I know. And I appreciate you going today. But her birthday is tomorrow, her last birthday, and her son is taking her out to a nice dinner, so she wants to get a new dress."

"Yeah, I get it. And you're welcome."

She kissed him, her long, streaked hair moving away from her shoulders.

"Hey, Bucko, you never know, but there could even be more in it for you tonight, you get it?"

"Now that's an interesting thought. But we just did it about three months ago," he said.

She kissed him again. "Well, let's step up our game."

"Deal. If you can get it up, you can have it."

"John! But I do love a challenge," she said, laughing.

They reached Gladys's front stoop. Libby pulled the storm door open and turned the brass handle of the large wooden door. It was locked.

"Now that's odd, she told me last night she'd be expecting us."

"Let me try."

John reached for the handle and had the same result as his wife.

"Hell's bells," he muttered.

Moving along the porch to the large bay window, he shaded his eyes with both hands and leaned his face against the glass.

The dust from the window irritated his eyes. He stepped away, pulled the handkerchief from the back pocket of his khaki shorts, and wiped his face. He squinted and looked again, his eyes growing larger.

Nothing. No Gladys and not even a sign of that annoying rat-dog she kissed like a long-lost grandkid.

"Damn it. Stay here. I'll go around to the side door. She has that key in one of those fake rock containers," said John.

"I better go with you. You'll be a month figuring out which rock is real and which one isn't."

"True dat," he said, in his best Hip-Hop impersonation.

She rolled her eyes. "You just aren't right."

They grasped hands and walked around the east side of the house toward the screened side door.

As they turned the corner, John noticed Gladys's dog lying on the ground, chewing something. Daisy's usually white face was a deep scarlet and, with her front paws, she held tight to whatever she was chewing.

They stopped in their tracks, Libby turning away.

"Ohh. I hate that blood stuff. Go see what she's eating."

"All right. All right. Fart. I suppose I'll have to."

John reluctantly shuffled in Daisy's direction.

As he got closer, she began to growl and became louder with each step he took.

His walk then ended abruptly, his heartbeat instantly pounding in his chest as he bent closer to make sure of what he was seeing.

The Pomeranian growled again, but he could now clearly tell that she wasn't chewing on a dead snake or a squirrel. That would have been acceptable. Instead, little Daisy was gnawing on a scorched human foot.

John turned and moved as fast as his legs would allow toward Libby, grabbing her hand as he went by her.

"John? What's wrong?"

"Just dig that cell phone out of your pocket."

She did, and then grabbed his arm, anxiety and fear on her face.

"I asked you a question."

"You did. Let's just say that I don't think we'll be going shopping today."

"Why?"

"Cause I don't believe Gladys is going to make it without a foot."

Her eyes grew wide as she stood closer to him.

He took the phone from her slender fingers and dialed 911.

As he waited for a connection, he found himself wishing to all of heaven and earth he'd played golf.

CHAPTER-11

The sun rose higher in the morning sky, and Manny adjusted his amber-lensed sunglasses a little tighter to his face, the warmth already piercing through the windshield of the unmarked SUV.

South Florida wasn't exactly known for its cold weather. Late spring here only drove that point home. It was going to be a hot one.

The unit, furnished by the local FBI office, was one of a three-auto convoy that had driven west of Miami proper on 90 and was now heading north on 997 along the very eastern edge of Everglades National Park. While the purpose for this trip was appalling, the view was captivating.

There was a distinct beauty in and around Northern Michigan, especially from the beginning of spring to the end of fall with its hundreds of miles of lakefront beaches and trails and the countless green trees and foliage topped off with the scent of native flowers like lilacs and seasonal roses. And there wasn't anything quite like Big Mac, the Mackinaw Bridge.

But this landscape of the low country, the Everglades, held an unmatched beauty and mystery of its own. The vegetation, especially the hanging moss, seemed alien to a northern boy like himself.

The green, lush swamp flora hid shallow pools of dark water which entertained a teeming fauna ecosystem as diverse, sensitive, and complicated as any. And of course, king in this environment was the alligator.

The north had nothing remotely close to this misunderstood predator, and there was a side of Manny that wanted to get close to one in the wild. Well, maybe not too close.

Shifting in the seat, he ran his hand through his hair.

Among all of this beauty, this untainted wildlife reserve, was a spot where the killer had chosen to murder his victims. He'd bound them to an innocent, ancient West Indies mahogany tree and carved them up like a butcher preparing for the day's business.

Author Randy Thornhorn was quoted as saying, "Can there be any question that the human is the least harmonious beast in the forest and the creature most toxic to the nest?"

He had that entirely right.

"You did the hand-through-the-hair thing. So what's going through that mind of yours?"

He glanced over at Sophie, who was driving the white SUV, styling as usual.

"Too many things I'm afraid."

"What the hell does that mean?"

"Nothing. I just sometimes struggle reconciling the ugly side of humanity with the nature around us, especially here. I like the Everglades. To kill two people here the way this asshole did violates more than one law in my book."

"So he's starting to piss you off?" asked Josh from the back seat.

"Could be. But like I always say, we have to take the emotion out of these cases and do our jobs."

"Okay, Great Sage of the North, we'll try to keep that in mind until we catch this prick, and maybe we won't beat him lifeless with a lead pipe or some shit," said Sophie.

"I'll help," said Dean, sitting beside Josh.

"That's two of us," said Belle, riding between Josh and Dean.

"You three aren't helping. But if we need a fourth . . ." said Josh.

The thought of taking this killer to task, seriously to task, had been lurking at the corners of Manny's mind all morning, fueled by a less than subtle anger that was becoming harder to control. At least these four could verbalize it. Mentally, he had to go in another direction or he'd join in on the conversation . . . and mean it.

What the hell is wrong with you, Williams?
You've been angry before. Get it together.

The scripture regarding God and vengeance he'd heard a time or two came to the forefront of his thinking. He briefly wondered if God ever needed help in that arena.

The next moment, the two squad cars in front of them made a quick left onto a small one-lane trail that barely doubled as a road. It continued for about a half mile before Sophie whipped in behind the two green-and-whites and brought the truck to a stop. They had pulled off near a small clearing surrounded by tall pampas grass and green mahogany saplings.

Manny's first thought was that this area was definitely secluded enough to do what Valentino had done. The man obviously knew that and took advantage of local knowledge.

Detective Marie Swifton exited the car on their right.

She was as tall as he remembered, slightly overweight, and a pretty woman with a dark complexion and sun-streaked black hair. She'd had a bit of an attitude the last time they'd met. Manny sensed none of that now, particularly after her warm greeting at the airport.

Her partner, Duane James, an over-sixty gentleman with curly gray hair, who stood as tall as Marie, got out of the other side of the car and moved next to her.

Three blues got out of the other unit and quickly positioned themselves across the semi-road they'd just entered, guarding it against an interruption Manny knew would never show.

Josh led the way from the vehicle as the BAU gathered in front of the two detectives.

"Are you ready for this?" asked Marie.

"We are," said Josh. "Even though your folks have already gone over the area, Dean and Belle have their forensic kits and cameras for another look from their angle. And Sophie and I have Williams."

"I think you have that wrong," said Sophie. "I think he's got us, you know."

"I'm not sure what that means," said Manny.

"In my weird-ass thinking, it means we're all in this together, got it?"

"You can explain that better to me later. Right now, let's get to it," said Manny.

"I think I agree with Manny, but I'd like to hear your reasoning as well, when we have time after we catch this scumbag," said Marie, offering a wry smile.

The two Miami detectives led them past another bank of high grass infiltrated by a row of squat palms with wide leaves. Then they moved into a smaller clearing decorated with yellow crime scene tape. It circled an area of about one hundred fifty feet. In the middle of that was the tree featured in the file photos he'd reviewed on the jet.

The tree was larger across and more majestic than Manny had imagined. It reminded him of a great tower rising from a forsaken green wasteland he'd seen in some fantasy movie.

"It really doesn't stand out from the road, does it?" said Manny.

Duane shook his head. "No, it's blocked quite well, but if you focus on it, you can sort of pick it out from 997. But when you get this close, it's special."

"Good God. Are you two members of the Arbor Club? What the hell difference does that make?" asked Sophie.

"Think, Sophie. Why would that be important?" asked Manny.

She started to speak and then stopped, rolling her eyes as if to say *oh yeah, let's get to work.* Manny could see her wheels were now turning in the direction this investigation needed.

Sophie folded her hands together and looked at the ground, then looked back toward Manny.

"It might not mean anything. But the tree and its location could be symbolic for how he sees himself."

"And how would that be?" asked Manny.

"Majestic and hidden away from everyone for the most part. What did Duane say, special?"

"Good thought. I think that could be true. In light of what we discussed on the jet and shared with Marie and Duane, this unsub thinks of himself as one of a kind, or certainly close to that.

He doesn't care for ordinary. I think he believes in the extraordinary and loves being next to it."

"So he sees this tree as some sort of experience with greatness?" asked Sophie.

"You mean like a sports or music groupie?" asked Josh, wiping the sweat from his brow.

"Sort of, but with a far deeper commitment," said Manny. "I think he believes he has something special to offer, something way out from the conventional, away from the run of the mill, a gift maybe."

"A gift of what?" asked Belle, setting her case on the ground.

Manny didn't answer; instead he put on his polyurethane shoe protectors and ducked under the yellow tape.

He moved closer to the tree, where the crimson blood stains were still clearly outlined in various patterns on the wide trunk.

Slowly circling the tree, he scanned it from the base to where the blood stains stopped at about seven-feet high. He was careful to not touch, even though he wanted to reach out a few times and pull things from the tree. He suspected . . . no, he *knew* Dean and Belle would find evidence that the Miami-Dade CSU hadn't. They were supposed to. Because they were the best of the best.

Finishing his lap around the tree, he stepped back about three feet and did it again, carefully changing his eye level and going over every square inch.

After a third round another yard farther away from the hardwood, he stopped, cocking his head to the left then to the right. He paced slowly to where the two bodies had hung together at their closest point.

Then he finally saw the haunting pattern created by Valentino.

"You all need to see this," he said without looking in their direction.

They gathered near him, looking over his shoulder.

"See what? I don't see crap," said Sophie.

"Belle asked about 'a gift of what?' I thought that a great question because I was thinking in a different direction."

"What direction?" asked Marie.

"I was thinking he thought of himself in narcissistic terms. That he was self-indulgent and above others. That he was entitled to do whatever he wanted to whomever."

"You don't think that now? I mean this reeks of an organized serial killer that has probably been forced to bone his sister or mother or uncle and he's ready to play out his revenge and frustration," said Marie, impatience in her voice.

"I don't. I think he's about something entirely different. Look closely at where these two stains meet, and then go right around the tree. Pretend you're looking at one of those image challenges we see sometimes that are like frogs and women in the same image, depending on how you focus your eyes. What do you see?"

It took them awhile, but one by one, with Belle being the first one to circle the tree, they each saw what Manny had discovered.

The collective release of pent-up breaths seemed to be in complete sync before anyone spoke.

"What a sick bitch," said Sophie softly. "What in hell does VALENTINO IS FREE mean?"

CHAPTER-12

The screeching din was louder than he'd thought it would be. But then again, he'd never really been this close to four police cruisers with lights flashing and sirens blasting in all of their magnificent glory.

He doubted most people had, unless they lived in one of the violent sections of downtown Miami. In that case, he supposed people would just keep doing what they were doing or rollover and go back to bed if the point of attention didn't concern them. It was truly interesting what people became accustomed to seeing and hearing. He knew that from personal experience.

Walking at just the right speed, flipping his lighter open and closed as he did, he moved down the sidewalk toward the house that had attracted so much attention.

The hot sun felt good on his back, and the faint scent of snapdragons riding along the breeze only heightened his sense of being totally alive. Finally.

He suddenly remembered visiting a butterfly house in Aruba as a child when he and his parents had traveled the Caribbean.

The creatures were amazing in themselves, floating and dodging everything that wasn't relevant to their world at that moment. So carefree. Except, of course, the occasions when a stray salamander got into the house.

During that visit, he'd watched a beautiful, vivid green malachite emerge from the ugly cocoon that had been its home for months.

It had been wondrous to him that something so unattractive had given birth to a creature so diametrically opposite of that ugliness. The creature was stunning.

From that moment forward, he longed to be engulfed in and subsequently released from that apparent paradox. His longing had finally ended. He had arrived.

It had taken time. Patience. Deep, reflective journeys into his upbringing as it related to his design, his ultimate gift and purpose. But in the end, like the butterfly, he sensed when the timing was right to escape the cocoon. To seek and embrace the freedom of becoming who he truly was.

Stopping a couple hundred feet away from the house, he closed his eyes, reflecting on the morning's activities. He'd been creative, a true artist in the creation of the display at the tree in the Everglades, but Gladys and her son Peter . . . well, that had been another step in his evolution altogether.

He wondered if the people who saw his creation would feel the same way. It was extremely difficult not to want to hear what they had to say. To see the looks of thoughtful expression as they commented on his talent. What artist didn't live for that?

Moving a bit slower, he finally reached the yellow tape encircling the house. The short, African-American female officer standing guard on that section of the sidewalk raised her hand for him to stop.

"Good morning officer. What's going on?"

"There's been a home invasion," she said.

"Oh no. Is everyone all right?"

"No. They are not. But you already know that, right?"

Her comment caught him totally off guard. He fought the panic rising from the bottom of his gut and the almost-overwhelming impulse to run.

How did they know? What had given him away? He'd been so careful, so true to his mission.

"What do you mean?" he asked, managing to keep his emotion in check.

She shook her head. "You know, the news station has had the information on the Internet before we even got out here, right? Damn Web anyway."

The rush of relief almost made his knees weak.

Getting caught was not on his dance card, but if that was going to happen, he wanted to express his love a few more times first. Check that. *Many* more times first.

"I must confess, you've got me there. I'm a bit of an online news freak."

"Yeah, well, how they got the scoop on what this sick son of bitch did is beyond me. Next thing you know, there'll be pictures posted of the crime scene," she said.

A sudden flash of pure rage took over his thoughts. Sick son of a bitch?

Again, he was fully aware that the police wouldn't appreciate his skills because, in their world, he was breaking the law. But to not appreciate the gift he'd offered exclusively to them was a different story. He'd thought that, above all others, law enforcement would appreciate his art.

Sick? He'd never been better. The shade of anger he was feeling was hard to ignore.

"Oh my, wouldn't that be something?" he asked.

The woman tilted her head and began to scan him from head to toe.

"Do you live around here, Mister . . .?"

"Vee. Mister Vee. And I do. Just around the corner on Stony Brook."

She smiled. "Well, Mister Vee, would you mind if we stopped by to ask you some questions?

Sometimes people see things that are important but don't really seem that way at the time."

"You mean like strange people and vehicles? Of course, officer, anything I can do. The house number is two-two-five-zero. I'm home during the day, mostly."

She opened her mouth to say something else, but the sound of loud voices coming from a group of neighbors caused the woman to turn from him and head back toward the house.

Turning around, he sauntered back the way he'd come, his mind racing with new concepts.

He wasn't sure what the people who lived at that address on Stony Brook would say to the cops when they stopped by for a chat, for one. How about when the cop tried to describe how he looked when she realized she'd been lied to, for another? Would she realize she'd been speaking to Valentino? He thought yes.

Yet neither of those ideas held a candle to what he was about to do next. He could thank the officer for the idea of how to expand his fan base. In fact, he might just have to do that in person. Maybe her boyfriend or husband would want to join him in the coming discussion.

If he were a betting man . . .

Reaching his car, he pulled away from the shaded side street and drove in the opposite direction from the house that would be forever enshrined as Peter's and Gladys' fifteen minutes of fame, thanks to him.

Yet, if the cops thought that he was a sick son of a bitch and didn't appreciate what he was offering to his exclusive audience, then what?

It didn't take a genius to see that his work would never be made available to the public, which in the beginning was a far thought from his mind. He had only wanted someone to recognize his gift, only wanted to show his brilliance to someone who would recognize him for what he was, and to show his unselfish love.

But if that need, and he did recognize it as such, wasn't going to be realized, then he had little choice but to go a different direction, one that would benefit artists and art connoisseurs alike.

"There are other methods to the desired results," he whispered.

CHAPTER-13

"Shit. Okay. We'll be there."

Marie put her phone back on her belt, her short hair moving in counter-rhythm with her shaking head as she walked back to the rest of the group, shaking her head.

Here we go, thought Manny.

"And I thought we had issues the last time you were down here," she lamented, making eye contact with Josh, then Manny.

"Another one?" asked Manny.

"Yes. A son and mother."

He could see from her face that there was more behind her answer.

"How bad?" he asked.

"Bad. Two of the officers left the scene, after puking their guts out, and four more refuse to go near the master bedroom suite. They said we don't pay them enough."

"Great. He's now not just a serial killer with some kind of screwed-up, delusional look at life, but a spree killer as well," said Duane James.

"Technically, he's a spree killer. Yet, I'm not sure of that," said Manny. "But I agree with your other assessment."

"What do you mean?" asked Duane.

"I'm talking about how he looks at his life. Who can define a cooling off period for a serial killer? People like us? I think that's up to the killers themselves. Is it five days? Six months? Twelve hours? Above that conjecture in this case, I don't believe this killer thinks of himself as hot or cold or whatever. He thinks of himself as free from whatever constraints he had previously."

"Okay, I see your points. We have to think outside the established norm for this guy," said Duane. "But it looks like a spree to me, and that means more bodies."

"I think we have to think like that with all of these cases because the perps hear a whole different type of music than the rest of us," said Josh. "And we have to stop him before we find more bodies."

"Listen, we can talk about the logistics of vocabulary and more victims later. I'd like to get to the new scene ASAP," said Manny.

"Are we going to talk about this message, how he did it, and what the hell it means first? We'd better because it's sort of freaking me out. How can he write so precisely and in such detail with something like blood and then pull off the effect like that?" asked Sophie.

"We've got to get to the new scene, but I'll ask you the same question. Other than the obvious perversion of what he did and how, who has this kind of ability?" asked Manny.

"I'd say someone who has a proclivity for arts and lettering, so maybe an art student or teacher. Or someone who might make a living drawing, painting, or whatever else those folks do," said Josh.

"Oh, right. Maybe even someone who owns or runs a studio," said Sophie.

"Yes, good guess on all accounts," said Manny. "Maybe even a graphic artist. This guy uses the same lettering type and is remarkably consistent. That says talent and practice to me."

"That makes perfect sense. We'll get to work on compiling a list of schools, colleges, and studios and get staff out there to start the interviews."

"Before you do, there's something else we should consider, an element that might narrow down the search."

"Damn. This is going to be sick, isn't it?" asked Sophie.

Manny shrugged. "We've seen enough things in this job, and outside of it, to know that one case of normal doesn't apply to all."

"So what should we be looking for?" asked Marie.

"There are and have been artists over the years that paint with their own blood, Vincent Castiglia from Hell's Kitchen in New York, also known as Doctor Rev, is pretty famous for that style. His work is creepy enough, but throw in the element of his own blood as the creative media and you have something truly eccentric," said Manny.

"I've seen his work and eccentric is a mild term. It's freaking creepy," said Dean.

"Really? You've seen his work? You're sleeping in another hotel room tonight," said Sophie.

"I said I've seen it. I didn't buy any, yet," said Dean, winking at Sophie.

"Yeah, hell will freeze over first before you hang that shit in our house."

"So we should look for locals who paint with blood?" asked Marie.

"Certainly. But not only that. I'd inquire regarding anyone who . . . well, has a different idea of just exactly what art is, and unusual media too," said Manny. "It may not lead to anything, but it's a start."

Marie exhaled. "I'll take a start, no matter how weird it is. Duane?"

"I'm on it," her partner answered. He then hurried toward the parked cars.

"All right. Let's get this sideshow on the road," Josh said. "I'll stay here with Dean while he processes the area. Manny, Sophie, and Belle, you go with Marie to the new murder scene. We'll meet at Marie's office in, say, four to five hours?"

"That works," said Manny.

He looked at Belle, and it occurred to him that she'd kept to herself during the last conversation. That wasn't like her.

She must have felt his eyes because she glanced in his direction, offering him a sad, if not nervous, smile. He felt as if she wanted to tell him something, but wasn't quite to the point of sharing yet, maybe not mustered enough courage. That thought alone was odd because she didn't appear to be afraid of many things.

"You okay with that, Belle?" he asked.

"Well, since you're asking. I'd like to stay here with Josh, if that's okay with all of you. I see some things that I'd like to take a closer look at," she said.

"Dean?" asked Manny.

"Sure, whatever she wants. I'm flexible. Besides, that would mean I can ride in the back with Sophie, you know?"

"I'll be driving. But if you want to sit in the front and put your hand on my leg, that works."

"TMI, from both of you. Okay, that's settled. And for the record, Williams is riding in the front. You three can take the SUV, after I get my sunglasses out of the back. We'll ride to town with the blues when we're done. Let's get to it," said Josh.

Josh headed for the SUV, Dean and Sophie right behind. Manny waited until they were out of hearing range then went to Belle.

"You okay?"

"Yep. I guess I'm still making adjustments, that's all."

"I understand that. But you know you can't bullshit a profiler, right?"

Her eyes danced, accompanied with a wide grin. "Can't blame a girl for trying though."

"Nope."

"You are good, no doubt about that. What gave me away?"

"I'm not sure about that good thing. I just pay attention. So what's bothering you?"

She touched his arm, her expression strong. "I appreciate your concern. I really do. And I'll make you a promise. Once Josh and I are done with this crime scene, and I'm satisfied with what we find, we'll talk."

"Fair enough. There's no pressure, just an offer to talk. These types of murders can rot your mind."

"Oh, I couldn't agree more, and thanks."

Belle released his arm, reached for her case, then limped over toward the tree.

He turned to go, then it struck him. He reversed his direction and moved to where Belle was opening her case.

She looked at him quizzically. "What? Do my pants have a hole in them?"

"No, none that I noticed. I have just one question for you before I leave though."

"Fire away."

"How did you injure your leg?"

Belle glanced away under the pretense of digging though her case. "I was injured on a trip. And I don't want to talk about it now."

"Another time then."

"Maybe."

Manny headed for the SUV, getting the answer he'd expected but seeing more.

Belle Simmons had a secret to share. An important secret.

CHAPTER-14

"How are you feeling?" asked Barb.

"Good, and wow, this is like a déjà vu moment. Do you remember the last time we were here at Walter Reed?" asked Alex.

"Oh, I sure do. Getting lucky in the closet while I was wearing the nurse get up. How could I forget that?"

"Ahh, well, that part was totally unforgettable and as far as I know, there was no security video showing what happened."

"There isn't. I checked."

Alex scowled. "Checked where?"

"The Internet. I looked through a bunch of porn sites having to do with nurses and didn't see us."

"You were looking at porn?"

"Sort of. I just wanted to make sure we weren't rising stars. But I'd be a liar to say I didn't enjoy some of it. Some of those guys are well . . . you know."

"I think Sophie would say 'hung'," said Alex.

She sat on the edge of the bed and kissed him. "She would, but she doesn't know about you, does she?"

"Not unless you told her during all that woman-talk thing you ladies do."

She zipped her fingers across her lips. "Some things are off limits."

Alex studied his wife. She hadn't grown a day older, it seemed, over the last ten years. Her platinum hair and striking features were enough to make anyone believe she was a famous actress or a model. She wasn't either of those things, and she loved him for some ungodly reason.

"What are you staring at?"

"You. Always you."

Kissing him again, she then ran her finger down his left arm to the fleshy stub that began where his hand had been.

"There's not much more to say about this, but I just want to make sure you're comfortable about this surgery."

Good question. Was he?

He'd run the various options over in his mind a million times and always came back to one conclusion. He had to do it this way. He could have finished his life with the other prosthetic, but this new technology would offer him far more, if things went right.

"I am. I'm excited to see where it will lead. And I can't wait to pinch Lee with fingers that are supposed to feel like the real deal."

Barb nodded. "That will be a Kodak moment."

Alex glanced at the wall clock. Twenty minutes until they came to get him. His stomach jumped at the thought. He wasn't sure if it was excitement or anxiety. Probably both.

"Well, I'd better go. They'll be here soon," said Barb, reading his face, no doubt. "Do you need anything else?"

He suddenly remembered that he did.

"I do, kind of. Last year, before Josh and I flew to Vegas, he gave you a piece of paper with an address and sent you there. I remember you had this big grin on your face when he told you that you'd know what to do when you got there. What was that all about?"

Her face grew somber. "I'm not really sure what you're talking about. I don't remember that."

He was no profiler, but he recognized a lie when he saw one, and lies were rare animals in Barb's world. Maybe she didn't remember. It was possible, right?

"Really? You don't remember? Josh said he had something else for you to do when you wanted to come with us."

Her face grew more taut. "Listen, Alex. I don't have any idea what you're talking about. Are you calling me a liar?"

"Of course not. I just distinctly remember that situation and was curious, that's all. It popped into my head just now for some reason."

"Well, I don't remember what you are talking about, and surely I would. Maybe it was the pre-surgery medication."

It had been a long while since they'd actually fought, and he didn't think this was the time to go down that path.

He smiled.

"Okay, I was a little drugged up. I was probably imagining things."

Her expression softened. "You're right. You were. But you've got more important things on your mind, so let's drop this."

Just then, the ER prep team entered the room.

"We're going in a bit early. So, if you're ready, let's get to this," said the tall doctor leading the procession.

"Sure, I'm ready, I think," said Alex.

Barb hugged him and pecked him on the cheek, but her usual warmth was missing, or at least it seemed that way.

She then walked out of the door.

The team rolled him out a few minutes later, and Alex was grateful for what was to come, his mind shifting away from the awkward conversation with his wife. He was going to be as close to normal as technology could muster, and that would be a dream come true, he prayed.

*****

Barb Downs watched as they rolled her husband down the hallway, thinking of their last conversation. She knew she hadn't really fooled him. He was a kind man who'd chosen not to call her out on her obvious lie. That kindness and soft-heart approach was a good trait, but it hadn't always served him well. Like today.

Then again, his day wasn't going to end like he, or the rest of the BAU, expected.

Not by a longshot.

CHAPTER-15

Manny ducked under the yellow ribbon and walked up the red stone path that led to the front door of the neat, white ranch. Dean was on his left, Sophie on his right, Marie led the way.

They entered the small foyer, moved past the two cops standing guard, and stopped in the middle of the open living room.

Immediately, the distinct scent of smoke and burnt wood invaded his senses, stopping him dead.

The chill that ran down his spine confirmed what he detected underneath those two odors. He'd been exposed to that deplorable scent only a couple of times in his career as a cop and special agent, but like his first murder case, he'd never forgotten it. No one in their right mind could.

Burnt flesh was like hell on earth.

"Is that what I think it is?" asked Sophie.

"I pray it isn't," said Dean.

Manny didn't think their prayers were going to be answered this time.

Marie echoed his thoughts. "I think you might be a little late on the prayer side of things. Follow me."

They moved over the immaculate hardwood floors, which were complimented nicely by the light blue leather furniture making a semi-circle around the large flat screen TV hanging on the wall. On each side of the TV and also on the adjoining wall leading to the kitchen were at least fifteen pictures of Gladys Blanks and her family from over the years. It was impossible to sit in either of the chairs or sofa and not see them. Gladys had obviously liked to reminisce.

The living room was cozy and could have been a special place for Gladys and her son. He could almost hear them ruminating and laughing as they spoke of the past with fondness.

His heart broke a little, and he silently thanked God for that part. It meant he still had a heart that worked.

On one of the recliners, near the right arm, were two numbered yellow markers tented up near three streaks of blood.

He followed Dean as he stepped over to the sofa, where four more markers, two near what looked to be characters burned into the leather. The other two gave attention to small piles of what appeared to be ash.

"Shit. I do this why?" asked Sophie, covering her nose with one hand, crossing her breasts with the other.

She glanced at Manny. "I know, I know. One of us says that every time we get to a new scene, but I mean it today. I'm getting tired of this junk. Not to mention, whatever's in the back of this house is going to make me want to do heavy-duty drugs again, isn't it?"

"Maybe, and we'll all probably want to join you. But there's only one way to find out for sure," said Manny.

With that, he walked past Marie, who had no qualms about letting him take the lead, and entered through the wide hallway leading out of the living room to the rear of the house. The stench of charred human flesh grew stronger, almost blotting out his ability to concentrate.

He held his nose as he passed the lighted bathroom to his right and another bedroom on the same side, then came to semi-closed French doors ten feet to the left.

With gloved hands, he gently pushed the two doors the rest of the way open. He took one step inside, something he immediately regretted.

At first, he thought he heard himself catch his breath, but it wasn't him. He was still holding his air in.

It had been Sophie. She had followed him directly into the room, and this time, his usually loquacious partner said nothing, the sight before them guaranteeing a horrific silence for the immediate future.

For one of the few times in his professional life, he seriously considered walking out, turning in his credentials, and calling it a career. The total revulsion and ambiance of this room demanded it. No one should be a part of this perversion, cops or otherwise. But he wouldn't leave, not today. They had to stop this version of pure evil that even Hollywood hadn't yet dreamed up.

Leaning provocatively against the post of the king-sized bed, hands taped to the rear left bedpost, lay what was left of a naked Peter Blanks. Sections of his body were burnt so badly that he looked like a piece of meat that had fallen into the flames of a barbeque.

The killer had been careful not to burn every part of his body. He'd left patterned sections of his arms, legs, and torso free from fire. The body resembled a huge, winding chessboard.

The contrasting squares of burnt flesh and unmarred flesh ended just below his chest where "VALENTINO" had been burnt in perfect letters, matching exactly, in Manny's eyes, the lettering they'd seen at Everglades Park.

Between the chest and the forehead were smaller checkered squares running up to the bridge of Peter's nose. They stopped, but only to allow for another rendition of "VALENTINO" printed across his forehead.

Peter's eyes caught Manny's attention—because they were missing, looking for all the world as if they'd been burnt from their sockets.

Resting between his splayed legs were three neatly aligned items. None of them particularly dangerous in themselves, but all were disturbingly ominous in this environment.

A blow torch, what appeared to be a commercial wood-burning tool, and a large plastic container of lighter fluid.

No genius was required to know what Valentino had done with those items.

As unnerving and revolting as Gladys' son's body was to look at, Peter wasn't the crème de la crème in this room.

Gladys Blanks hung from the room fan, almost directly over her son, her body also void of clothing and charred in similar fashion to Peter's, only the squares were more difficult to see against her darker frame. She possessed both signature VALENTINOs lettered in the usual places on her chest and forehead.

The old woman's arms were spread wide, like Jesus addressing His children in several popular paintings, each arm forced into that position by what looked like small pieces of wood, attached, somehow, at her thin sides and just under her biceps.

The appearance of hovering over her son was horrible enough, but there was an added element to this setup from the first scene in the

Everglades, other than the fact that half of the room had been torched and singed to varying degrees.

Valentino hadn't removed her eyes, rather had placed a pair of exotic, Elton John-like glasses over them, minus the lenses. The angle of her head and the placement of the glasses gave the appearance of a painting with eyes that followed one around the room.

Was there anything beyond the appalling imagination of a killer such as this?

Manny, unfortunately, knew the answer to that.

He released his pent-up breath. "God in heaven," he whispered.

"I think I'd equate this more with Satan in hell, if he exists," said Dean.

Marie and Dean had moved near to the opened doors of the room and stood just behind Sophie.

"How can you see this and think he doesn't?" said Marie, turning away.

"Is the devil even this perverted?" asked Sophie, joining her.

Doing everything within his power to get his head away from the emotion and back into cop mode, Manny moved closer to the bodies.

"I think that's a topic for another discussion. We have to get to work and stop this lunatic before he takes another step into his world."

"Just like that? You turn off this nightmare shit and say get to work?" asked Marie.

"If you don't, you'll be in rehab and knitting scarfs for the poor," said Sophie.

"She's right," said Dean. "You have to realize that they're gone, and these bodies are not who they are or were. Our job is to find who checked them out."

"I get that, but . . . but . . . never mind. What do you want me to do, Manny?" Marie asked, her voice gradually becoming steadier.

"Thanks for asking. We'll need more time to get ready for the meeting this afternoon, and we'll have more information and more requests as we process this room, but for now, we need all of the usual bases covered."

"I don't even know what the usual is in this situation," said Marie.

"Let's start with cell phone and landline records of these two and see if they have any connection with the first two vics. Who knows? Maybe there's a common number that links all of them."

He ran his hands through his hair, then continued,

"We need credit card and bank records. Job information. Charity giving, social club affiliations, and any social media associations. Vacations and travel. We need to talk to relatives and neighbors, again," said Manny.

Looking around the room, it came to him to look for something else, but he had a question first.

"Dean. What do you think the time of death was?"

Dean raised his bushy eyebrows and then stroked his beard. "That's tough to say. I mean we can use the thermometer-to-the-liver gig, but these bodies were exposed to heat and extreme temps. That will mess with accuracy."

Walking over to Peter's body, Dean kneeled and got close to his legs. He then stood and carefully eyeballed the suspended Gladys Blanks, then came back to Manny.

"There's some discoloration showing, even with the state of the bodies, due to rigor mortis. The ME will have a better idea than I do, but I suspect just a couple of hours before it was called in. Maybe eight a.m. or so. Why?"

He turned toward Marie. "We've established time of death with the other couple as around eleven p.m. About thirty-six hours ago, right?"

"Yes. So?"

"So," said Sophie, interrupting, "we need to know when they came up missing, right?"

"Right. I want to know the last time anyone had contact with them."

"You're seeing some symmetry here?" asked Marie.

"Maybe. If he killed these folks at or around eight this morning and the other victims came up missing about eight p.m., then it could give us insight to his timeline for the next victims."

"Thirty-six hours, then?" asked Sophie.

"If we're right, yes. He'll pull the trigger again in about thirty-two hours."

CHAPTER-16

"Is there anything else you want me to do?" Josh asked.

Belle shook her head. "No. Thanks for loading up all of those samples for me. Most of it will amount to busy work for the local lab, I suspect, but sometimes . . ."

"The little things lead to big things, yeah I know, thank God."

Belle nodded and then turned back to what she was doing and away from him.

His new hire had been avoiding eye contact almost the whole time since the others had left for the house in Miami. He understood working quirks. Max Tucker had had a few. Dean and Alex worked better when they were in each other's company. Sophie . . . well, Sophie was enigmatic, but effective. Then there was Manny, who had a process all his own, including spending time alone with the scene, if he felt it mandated that. Manny's intuition and insight were all about his feelings and a certain logic that supported those feelings. He at least understood what made these killers tick, if not how.

Yet, Josh wasn't at all sure about Belle and her methods, not entirely. She'd been a great help in Cozumel running down the Mayan copycat killer, showing a much lighter approach there than here in South Florida.

She'd displayed excellent profiling and forensic skills, just as advertised when he'd hired her. But something was bothering her here. No doubt Manny had already seen it—he always did—but for some reason, she hadn't talked to him, at least he didn't think so. If she had, and it was important, Manny would have told him.

It was time for big brother to take over.

He helped Belle as she rose from her knees after scrutinizing a blood-covered blade of grass stuffed in a polyurethane bag. She thanked him, then placed it on her thigh and wrote the date, the time, and the location on the tab, eventually placing it with another batch of bags.

She must have felt his stare because she met him eye to eye.

"What is it, Josh? You've been side-glancing me for two hours."

"I'm not sure. You'll have to tell me."

"I don't know what you're talking about. I'm fine."

But the quick glance to her hands said otherwise.

"Belle, listen. I'm no profiler. Hell, Sophie does a better job of that kind of thing when she focuses. I'm pretty much the administrative guy who doubles as your special-agent boss, but a few things have rubbed off hanging around with you folks. For example, my bullshit meter swung way to the right after you answered me just now."

She didn't want to, but Belle couldn't help but laugh, a deep belly laugh, her eyes dancing impishly as she did.

"You have a bullshit meter?" she asked, that mischievous twinkle still there.

"Oh yeah. I have two young boys with active imaginations. It's a built-in requirement for dads . . . and bosses, I might add."

Belle sighed, removed her gloves, and stuffed them in her back pocket, reaching down to rub her knee. When she stood straight up again, she folded her arms over her ample breasts.

"So Manny would tell me that excessive motion is a subconscious avoidance mechanism," said Josh. "And you've just run the full gamut from butt to knee to folding your arms. All after a sigh."

"He'd be right, on all accounts. You know, you keep saying you can't read people, profile or whatever term you want to use, but from the second we met, you've had a good idea about me. If I were you, I'd think a bit higher of my ability along that line," said Belle.

"Yeah well, that's where interviews, resumes, and psych exams come in handy too," said Josh.

"I suppose they do."

The brief silence, in Josh's estimation, readied them both for some revelation as to what had been bothering her.

"Belle, I want you to tell me what's going on with you."

After gazing out toward the edge of the Everglade's landscape for a full minute, she turned to Josh, rubbing the back of her neck.

"I can't be sure. It's been a long time since that day, but I may have seen this killer before."

CHAPTER-17

Little Ian had just stopped the latest round of bouncing on his granny's lap, the joy of his laughter unmatched and as whimsical as any music God offered to the planet. Laughing children could be the elixir that cured the world. At least that's what Chloe thought.

"The wee one can laugh, can't he?" said Haley Rose, then she engaged in another rousing round of pony express with Ian as the rider on her knee, the object of her full attention. He howled with glee, his mother and granny helpless not to join him.

"That he can. That he can. I think he gets it from his dad," she said.

"Ya might be right with that. He sounds like Manny, and that's not all the lad got from his father. He's got your hair, but those blue eyes and that face . . . well, no trouble guessing if the milkman came to visit or not."

"Mum! Besides, no milkman needed with a man like that sleeping in my bed."

Haley Rose laughed. It sounded almost as good to hear as Ian's own joy.

It was one of the few times she'd heard Haley Rose laugh since the incident when her mum's long-ago lover came from Ireland to the states to give them all a special taste of evil, ending with Jen shooting the psychotic man.

She didn't say so, she wouldn't, but Chloe knew her mum blamed herself for the ride the crazy man had taken them on, for forcing Jen's hand and ending an innocence that could never be recaptured.

But what could Haley Rose have done? Chloe knew as well as anyone that one person had no control over the actions of another. That kind of influence was reserved for God, and He was far too much a gentleman to force His will on others. Evil was always a choice. Thus the great battle of good versus evil.

Good Lord. Her thoughts were more Manny-like every day.

Haley Rose got out of the kitchen chair and handed Ian to Chloe, after one more kiss on his chubby cheek. Her mum sat back down and stole a long draw from her vanilla latte.

"I need to finish my coffee and get ready for Jen when she gets home."

Chloe smiled. The two of them were headed for another shopping trip to the mall, something that had helped to bond step-grandmother and stepdaughter in a true and loving relationship. "They are thick as thieves," Manny had said.

There were times in everyone's life—adult, adolescence, and especially childhood—that dictated a need for another individual, no matter the gender or age group, to help guide one through a rough time.

Over the last eighteen months, Haley Rose had lost two men with whom she'd built a special relationship, even though Doctor Argyle was far removed from a true man in Chloe's eyes. But Gavin Crosby had been a good man and that relationship could have gone somewhere, but for his untimely death in Las Vegas. Two daggers to the heart were obviously far worse than one.

Jen, so much like her dad, had lost her mother two and a half years ago. Louise had been a wonderful mother; and the two of them, mother and daughter, had been extremely close.

Chloe held no illusions that she alone could replace the irreplaceable, although she was giving all she had to that end. But the almost immediate bond between step-granny and stepdaughter had been impossible to ignore, and was certainly unexpected.

After all, what did an American teenager have in common with an Irish woman over fifty who'd traveled a tough, rocky road of her own?

Only God knew, and that should be enough.

"What are ya thinkin', girl?"

"Just how much I love seeing you and Jen spending time together. I know Ian's your first grandbaby by blood, and it does a girl's heart good to see the two of you together, don't you know. Jen and you . . . well, that's a great one."

"Aye, it is."

Chloe watched as her mum choked back a sudden attack of heart-twisting emotion, something Chloe was familiar with these days herself.

"The girl is so strong, so determined to not let life kick her young arse and tear out her heart. It makes me want to be better for her. That makes me better for me. She's a special one, she is. I didn't meet her mother, but Manny lives in that one."

"You have that right, Mum, all of it."

"I'd also be a liar if I told you she didn't want to make me fight for what I want too, even at my age."

Mother and daughter remained silent, even as Ian fidgeted on his mom's lap before finally giving in to the warmth and heartbeat of his mother. As he drifted to sleep, Chloe reached out and touched her mother's hand.

"Mum. Do you want to talk about it?"

"About what?" her mother asked, as if she had no idea. Her green eyes gave her away, however.

"About Ennis Preston and what he did," she said softly.

This time, there was no dodging the issue that was playing with both of their hearts. No side-stepping the prodigious elephant sitting on the round oak table or trying to ignore its ever-present odor. There was a certain, psychological stench associated with traumatic ordeals unresolved. Chloe knew how those situations worked. The scar on her calf from a terrorist's bullet was a not-so-subtle reminder of an unexpected encounter with her own mortality.

Her mum's eyes had turned to fire. "What would I talk about, child? Would I state the obvious, girl? That I hate that my past came back to bite young Jenny's mind and soul? That Ennis, crazy-ass Ennis Preston, almost killed my wee ones because of his twisted affection for me? That it would have given me sorrow without end to finally see you happy with a child and a family of your own and have it all destroyed if my grandgirl hadn't been her father's child and possessed the strength to shoot the bastard? That their deaths would have been all my damned fault?"

"Mum—"

"No. You listen to me now. I'll be quiet when I'm finished." Haley Rose closed her eyes, struggling for control.

It reminded Chloe of when she was a child and had done something wrong and her mum was deciding between a switch or something else as a means of lasting education.

Haley Rose opened her eyes, the fire diminished somewhat. "I think of what could have been almost every moment I'm awake and then some. I realize that none of the three of us would be here if things had gone down another road. It's what mothers like us do. I rack this old mind to see what I could have done differently, but in the end, it does me no good because I couldn't have done anything differently. Destiny, fate, or providence from Holy God are all involved in what happened, or none of them are—we can take our pick there.

"All I truly know is that we're here. Ian is safe. Jen is left pondering life and death, but safe. I'm beatin' the hell out of myself a few times a day, but we're safe, and none of us are the worse for wear, you kin?"

Chloe nodded, relieved that her mum was prying this monkey from her back.

She continued. "I know that you and Manny hold me no ill will, and I know that in my heart of hearts, not just from the words you've said to me. For that, I'm truly grateful. It has helped me cope with my own thoughts."

Haley Rose sipped her latte again. Chloe waited.

"So, I woke this fine mornin' and decided to take advantage of my new go at living a life. One for me."

Just then, Jen flew through the front door, pink backpack over her shoulder, her cell phone glued to her ear, a wide smile painted on her pretty face as she said goodbye to someone on the phone.

"Hey, you two," she said, rushing across the room to the kitchen. She then bent down and kissed her sleeping little brother, a sparkle in her hazel eyes as she gazed at him.

Looking up, she winked at her granny. "You ready for a big night at the mall?"

"So why is that any different than usual for us, child?"

Jen looked at Chloe then back to Haley Rose, her grin wider than a clown's mouth at a putt-putt golf course.

"Well, I may need a prom dress after all," she said, squealing and then putting her hand over her mouth as Ian groaned.

As if practicing some Vulcan mind-meld trick, the three of them held their breaths and stared at Ian, hoping he would stay asleep. He did.

"Did that Martin boy finally ask you?" asked Chloe, feeling excitement for Jen that could only be exceeded by her real mom's . . . and maybe her granny's.

"He did. Seth Martin, the hottest geek in all of Lansing, asked me to go to the prom during chemistry class. It was kind of . . . well, really romantic."

"Chemistry class now? Well, what took him so long?"

"I think Manny Williams, FBI special agent profiler, had something to do with it. I told Seth that Dad hadn't tortured and killed any teenage boys for years. He finally believed me."

They laughed as Jen skipped down the hall toward her room, Ian still sleeping soundly.

"There ya go," said Haley Rose after Jen's door had slammed. "She's alive and moving on."

"She is. It's great to see."

Exhaling, Chloe took her mum's hand again. "Are you good, mum? Are we good?"

"As right as rain. It'll storm a time or two, I reckon, but we'll be fine, all of us."

Good wisdom, thought Chloe. She also thought it time to ask one more question before they moved to the lighter side of life.

"So what did you mean when you said you're going to make a go at living a life for you?"

Haley Rose stood from the table and smiled at her daughter. "You'll just have to see now, won't ya?" She headed down the same hallway that Jen had just traveled, on the way to her room.

Chloe watched Haley Rose until she disappeared.

Her mum was going to live her life, words that Chloe and Manny had been waiting to hear, but for reasons she didn't understand, they'd left Chloe with a frown on her face and an unsettled feeling in her mind.

CHAPTER-18

Teamwork was essential to success in almost every endeavor known to man. Everyone doing his part made the world go around, in Manny's estimation.

Square pegs in square holes, round pegs finding the perfect partner, women and men finding their soul mates made for an easier life for all involved.

But none of those philosophical or practical ideas were any more important than in the crime-fighting arena.

Everyone had to do his job to the absolute best of his ability, revealing all he knew, not holding back even the quirkiest of ideas or thoughts, especially in a unit like the BAU. Even a workaholic Special FBI Agent knew that. That's why Manny pushed himself so hard during these investigations. That, and the idea that the victims, by definition, demanded justice.

It was also why he'd fought desperately to control his temper after Josh had called him to tell him that Belle may know something about this case and hadn't said anything earlier. Apparently, she told Josh that an event she'd experienced in her childhood reminded her of this killer.

Manny had known something was bothering her, yet he'd had no idea what.

He fought off the anger again.

An image of the man he'd pulled from that rusted chain-link fence in the musty alley in Lansing, then snapping his ankle, rolled to the front of his mind.

"Anger" and "good cops" should not mix, not even be used in the same sentence, he supposed. In fact, it was advice he'd given to many, a mantra to not merely practice but to live by.

Yet, here he sat in one of the smaller meeting rooms off of Miami-Dade's main conference room, contemplating the ramifications of shaking Belle so hard her bones would rattle.

He remembered what Gavin Crosby had told him a million times. "Easy boy, don't let this job make you a news headline."

But this work was making him a little crazy, wasn't it? He'd seen so much, and not just the physical—he'd dove deep into the forbidden waters of the serial-killer mind more than once. How much longer could he do that before something gave? He was only human, after all.

He shook his head and grinned to himself, his mood lightening. "Wow. Take it easy Williams, whining doesn't get it done," he said out loud.

Still, lighter mood or not, he understood he wasn't entirely without grounds for his pissy attitude. If Belle had been forthright with the team from the get-go, they would be that much closer to finding this screwed-up bastard. Hell, maybe they would even have him behind bars. Better yet, in the morgue.

But he also knew that people handle personal trauma and horrifying experiences differently. Some people tell everyone on the planet, which was far easier these days with the advent of the Internet. Many, however, kept traumatic events buried deep inside, often letting their minds hide from the reality of truth, repressing to the point that they never truly realize what had happened to them in the past.

Then there are those in Belle's boat. They remember. They allow that event to shape their lives on several levels, consciously or subconsciously. He'd bet part of the reason she became a cop was because of said incident, which he still knew nothing about.

The door swung open, hammering the wall with such force that Manny felt the table leg rattle.

He sprung to his feet, reaching for the Glock at his shoulder.

"I'm going to tell him first and that's the end of it."

"But Belle, you don't have to do it this way," said Josh, reaching for her as she advanced inside the room.

Belle swung around and struck like a cornered cobra. The quick slap on Josh's hand was notably loud, to put it mildly.

"You can touch me when I say you can. I need to talk to this man alone. Do you feel me?"

He'd seen some fearsome lightning in folks' eyes before, but the blaze coming out of Belle's eyes . . . Manny stepped back.

Josh stopped, his blue eyes wide. He looked at his hand, then to Belle, then to Manny, then back to his hand.

Up to that point in his life, Manny didn't recall ever using the word "flabbergasted" but nothing fit his boss's and friend's current state any better.

By then, Sophie and Dean had crowded around Josh, Sophie laughing so hard that tears streamed down her cheeks. Dean was an almost polar opposite, shock scripted deeply on his bearded face.

"Feel you? Is that what people say just before they get their ass fired for hitting their boss?" asked Josh.

"You do whatever the hell you want, Joshua Corner, but you ain't doing shit until I talk to Manny, alone. And . . . have I told you how much I hate repeating myself?"

Taking three long, staggered steps toward Manny, Belle stopped a foot away, scanning his face so intently that he had to tilt his head to get her attention.

She stood six inches shorter, but the fierceness of her body language combined with her obvious emotional state made her seem much taller.

That wasn't all. Sure, Belle was angry, almost in a rage, but that was only half of the story. This new member of the BAU also seemed frustrated and ashamed and embarrassed all in one. Manny guessed she had thought she had her motions under control. Cop control, he called it. But this case and her subsequent actions dictated otherwise. Control was and would always be an illusion, he suspected.

His own anger became a distant memory. Belle's current state reminded him that, above all else, the Guardian of the Universe was about people. All people, particularly the hurting. And this woman was in pain.

"We need to talk, Manny. I have to—"

Pulling Belle tight, he held her close even as she tried to pull away, then slowly, like sand slipping through an hourglass, she relented. She wrapped her arms around Manny. She shook for a moment, a tiny sob escaping into his chest.

"You don't have to do anything Belle. I get it. We all do. That's why we're a team," he said softly, cursing his own self-centered pity party from earlier.

About the people, Williams. Always.

He felt her nod, exhale, and then step back from him as Sophie, Dean, and Josh approached.

"You're some kind of people whisperer, Manny," she said, wiping her eyes. "I'm sorry I got so angry. I just wanted to smack Josh for calling you and telling you what I shared with him."

"From where I'm standing, I think you did that, the smacking part, I mean. That was sweet," said Sophie, grinning.

"It was damn loud too," said Dean.

Josh faked a horrified look at his red hand. "I'll not be able to use this again."

"Too bad. You'll have to spend more time with your wife now, won't you?" said Sophie, her grin even wider.

"Smartass," said Josh.

Belle laughed, which caused the rest of them to follow suit. Her mirth was a magical quality. Manny thought they could all do with more of that.

After reaching up to kiss Manny on the cheek, she motioned toward the faded veneer table. "Thank you all. Okay, it's time to get this mushy stuff behind us. I'm ready. Let's get to this," said Belle.

Dean closed the door and the five of them sat down, Manny across from Belle and Josh, Dean to his left and Sophie to his right.

"First of all, Josh didn't tell me much except that you may have some knowledge of this guy," said Manny.

Letting out a pent-up breath, Belle nodded. "It happened about twenty years ago. We were on vacation in Saint Kitts, as was the norm during the summer for my parents and me. My father loved the Caribbean way of life, and it was even a slower pace back then. As a teacher, he also loved the chance to spend time with the local kids. Mom and I spent a ton of time with him too, but the sun and sandy beach was what we held near and dear."

"I understand that one," said Sophie. "I need to work on my tan. God knows that didn't work out so well in Cozumel."

"I think you're perfect the way you are," said Dean.

"Oh man, how many more points can this boy earn?" asked Sophie.

"Later, you two. Actually not even later. I don't want to know anymore. Belle?" Josh waved for her to continue.

She nodded. "Good points for sure though. Anyway, I was thirteen, and this particular summer, we spent six weeks on the east side of the island at a small resort called Saint Kitts Palace. It had these little beachfront cabanas, small two-bedroom variety, maybe seven hundred square feet. You literally walked out of the front door to the beach and ocean sixty or seventy feet away."

"Sounds like heaven," said Manny.

"It was. The resort, cabanas and all, were lost in the hurricane of '99. Hurricane Lenny. They didn't rebuild and eventually sold out to a large resort corporation."

"Too bad," said Sophie. "We could have screwed up another vacation by booking there."

"Yeah, not much luck on the vacation front lately," said Manny.

Belle frowned. "It's funny how it made me feel when I found out the resort was gone. Childhood memories can be the best thing since white wine or the worst thing since grade B sci-fi movies."

"Hey, I like those," said Dean.

"That explains some things," said Josh.

"Go on, Belle," said Manny.

She shifted in her chair, folding her hands in front of her as she settled in.

"That year, 1997, I was growing into a young woman, and puberty was a bit confusing. I remember wanting to spend less time with my parents and more time with a couple of the local girls I'd known for four or five summers, Cammy and Trisha. They were about my age, both skinny with braided hair down to their shoulders and great white smiles, so we had a natural propensity to hang out with each other. Plus there were some really cute boys on the island, and I was starting to notice. I wanted to have someone my age to talk to about the things I was feeling." She grabbed a bottle of water sitting in the middle of the table and drank her fill then continued.

"These two thought that pretty funny because they'd both had boyfriends, on and off, from the time they were ten or so. At any rate, they helped me by having the kind of girl talks and laughs that I needed."

Belle reached for the water again, her hand shaking as she pulled it back. Manny wondered if she thought she would spill the water. He also knew she was getting to the gist of this experience. He felt his stomach flutter with anxiety for her. This wasn't going to be easy.

"During our last week, in fact on the thirty-first of July, Trisha showed up bright and early so we could walk along the old railroad tracks that circled most of the island and explore a couple of old caves running near Bloody Point. We wanted to see the bats and whatever else along the way. And the island was supposed to be so safe, so . . ."

Belle drifted for a moment, as if her mind's eye saw something totally different than this room and the people sitting in the padded chairs.

Licking her lips, she refocused and continued.

"Cammy was late, as usual, but she knew where we were headed, so we took off. It was quite a hike, maybe four or five miles from the beach, but we were up for it.

"We entered the rails from the southeast and began walking, laughing about silly things. Trisha always made fun of how I tried to say 'mon.' I picked on her because of her stick legs and big feet. The longer we walked, the more silly we got until it dawned on us that Cammy hadn't caught up with us. We thought maybe she'd gotten into trouble with her mom, again, and was grounded. We were wrong."

Swallowing hard, Belle reached for the water, and this time was able to remove the top and take another long draw.

She set it down, staring at the drops inside the bottle as they ran painstakingly to the bottom of the container.

"What happened, Belle?" asked Manny quietly.

She sighed. "We reached the area near the caves just after crossing one of the trestles that bridged a sixty-foot ravine and began the last part of our trek along the river. We were kind of pinched between high rock walls and the water, so eventually we had to take off our shoes and walk in the water. It felt cool and wonderful, smelling like fresh rain and was as clear as a cloudless night.

"We'd gone maybe two hundred feet when we came upon a shoe sitting on the muddy bank. It was white, but we noticed a red streak on the side that looked like paint. Trisha joked it was blood, trying to sound like Vincent Price. We laughed and kept going. We didn't think about it because it wasn't uncommon to find clothes and other things discarded along this trail.

"Turning around a bend, the foliage became heavier, and the sun was blocked by the rocks. It was still light enough to see clearly, but Trisha took the flashlight out of her backpack and shone it in front of us. We went another hundred feet and came to the entrance of the cave. Right where the water from the river met the rocks was the match for the other shoe.

"This time we stopped. It had gotten our attention because there were more red streaks on both sides of the shoe. It wasn't paint because the red was milking into the water. We knew it was blood. Worse, we simultaneously recognized the shoe as Cammy's.

"Immediately Trisha began moving into the cave, screaming Cammy's name. I never had the opportunity to ask her, but I think we both thought Cammy got there early to scare us or something then fell and hurt herself. It was the only plausible explanation.

"I followed Trisha into the cave but neither one of us got very far.

"A young white boy burst from the recesses of the cave, his khaki shirt and shorts covered in blood. He thrust an arm at Trisha, hitting her in the chest and sending her reeling. She hit the rocks hard, but caught herself and stayed up, yelping with pain just the same.

"The next thing I knew, that boy was swinging a knife, a big knife, probably a machete, directly at my head."

Belle looked at Manny, her face expressing and perhaps releasing the pain that had been torturing her for over twenty years. He felt her gaze to his very core, doing his best to control the shiver threatening his spine.

"Keep going, girl," said Sophie.

"Everything seemed to be in slow motion, as if time stood still or like one of those out of body experiences people talk about. It was like God wanted it to be that way. Anyway, for one brief moment, our eyes met. He was wearing a scarf around his face, so I didn't get a great look at the rest of him, but I'll never forget what was in the midst of those dark eyes.

"He was not, you know, excited or crazy or angry, or any other dark emotion you'd assume from someone who was swinging a blade at me, but calm, almost happy. It's hard to explain . . . like he was completely in his element and reveled in it.

"I ducked as I heard the knife swoosh over my head, slipping into the water as I did. He kept running and was out of sight in no time.

"Well, I got up, totally soaked from the river. Trisha stumbled to my side as, for some reason I can't explain, we focused on where he came from as opposed to where he was going. I guess we both knew something horrible had happened . . . to Cammy.

"We hurried into the cave, stooping low as we heard a bat leaving the dark, but not the least freaked out about a flying rat this time. The freak out began a few seconds later.

"Propped up against the side of the rocky cave
. . ." Belle paused and swallowed hard. "Just
inside the shadowy side, a stray stream of
sunshine running diagonally across her body, was
Cammy, her lifeless eyes wide open. Her clothes
were sliced but still on her body. Her throat was
sliced too, literally from ear to ear, still gushing."
Belle inhaled deeply, obviously struggling to stay
the course and finish telling what she'd not
spoken of for years, maybe ever. Manny was both
thankful she was telling this tale and appalled
there was such a story to share.

His stomach roiled even more.

Spreading her hand flat on the table, she
stared at them as she spoke.

"I'd never seen that much blood before. It's one
of those images we carry with us until God takes
us home."

"Trisha screamed and screamed then turned
and ran out of the cave. I didn't really know where
she lived and because of that, and maybe a dozen
other reasons, I never saw her again."

"I wanted to do the same, but for some
ungodly reason, I couldn't. I had no control of my
feet or legs, and even less of my eyes. I just
scanned her over and over. I supposed I was
fascinated, in a shocked sort of way. Cammy had
been a living, breathing young woman and now
she looked like a victim from a Freddie Kruger
movie."

"Were you concerned that the kid might come back?" asked Dean.

She shook her head. "No. I knew he was gone. Somehow, I knew. Maybe even then I suspected his job, or whatever the hell he wanted to call it, was completed.

"The blood and mutilation was bad, but slowly I realized there was a pattern to it. He'd carved into my friend's arms and one leg in loosely shaped rectangles that connected at the points. Three on each of three limbs. We probably scared him off before he finished, but then again, I'm not sure about that.

"My shock must have worn off about then because I ran out of the cave, sprinting as fast as I could. A few hundred feet down the river, I slipped on some wet rocks, dislocating and breaking my knee so horribly that five surgeries couldn't put me back together properly. I laid half in and half out of the water, screaming in agony for someone to help me, crying for more reasons than the pain in my leg.

"Finally, a local sugar cane farmer heard me and carried me to the tracks, where he flagged down a train.

"I told them, more like babbled inconsolably, about Cammy. It took a few minutes, but they got it and called the island police.

"As they loaded me into the ambulance, I recalled one more thing that I'd seen on poor Cammy's body."

"Which was?' asked Josh.

"There were two letters carved into her forehead just underneath her hairline, semi-covered by blood-matted hair. I obviously saw them, but it took time to register."

"Which letters?" asked Manny.

Belle pulled her hands off the table and began to rub her arms as if some arctic vortex had just waltzed into the room.

"NO. The letters were NO."

CHAPTER-19

"How are you coming on that Anderson project?"

Pulling his phone from his ear, he looked toward the sky. He knew most people had a boss, and granted, he had freedom that most only dreamt about. Then again, most people lacked his talent.

He could work from his home or from some shithole third world country or even go into the office and sit in a stale, worn-down cubicle and perform his magic. His *other* magic.

"Did you check your inbox, Fred? I sent it about three hours ago, along with the Meredith updates and the Schmidt revisions."

He heard the fat man clear his throat, probably after swallowing another dozen doughnuts.

"I . . . well, I hadn't gotten that far, meetings and all," he managed.

"Well, handle it, Fred. I've got other irons in the fire and can't be bothered because *you* didn't do your job."

"You can't talk to me like that; I'm your boss, dammit."

"Okay, well, I guess I can get work someplace else. I don't like the shit you're giving me here. I wonder what the Old Lady would say about that, Federico."

There was a delicious, pregnant pause. He actually heard Fred put something else in his mouth. He answered a moment later.

"It's a damn good thing you're the best graphic artist I've ever seen because you're an asshole, you know that?"

"Fred, how kind of you to say that. But you better apologize for the asshole remark or I'm in the wind, as they say, and you never know where I'll pop up. Maybe at the Clausen Agency. Now that would be a twist, wouldn't it? The Old Lady would have your nuts around your neck for letting your best go to hcr bitter rival, I think, don't you?"

The sound of more chewing caused him to smile.

"Okay. Okay. I'm sorry. I'm just under the gun and stressed here."

Another pause. Then Fred spoke again, desperation filtering in.

"You wouldn't really do that, leave us, right?"

"Just keeping my options open. I've got to go. And Fred, make sure you don't send me any work for a few days. I'm taking some 'me' time."

"No problem. I'll take care of you."

The big man hung up. The relief in Fred's voice made him laugh out loud.

"Keep them on a string, that's my motto," he whispered.

Putting the cell back into his shirt pocket, he crossed his legs underneath the café's outside table, sipped his espresso, and then touched the screen of his laptop. It sprang to life, showing an island drenched in sun.

Glancing up through his shades, he then closed his eyes in utter bliss.

The Florida sun was warm, hot even, and it felt good to him. It always had. But the sun was especially nice in the Caribbean. He knew about the Caribbean and what it had to offer, in several realms.

Going back to the screen, he stared at his next project, his next *personal* project, and was at a loss to control the sudden onset of true emotion. Tears welled up and then streamed down his tanned face.

Their rendezvous with destiny, with immortality even, was in his hands. He couldn't be more grateful and humbled at the same time to be the vehicle that would put them in that position. No one would forget them, if he was on top of his game.

That thought brought him full circle as he smiled again, brushing at the impromptu tears.

When had he not been at the top of his game?

The Roman numeral analog countdown clock flashed on the screen, displaying exactly twenty-six hours until he blessed the next couple with his abilities. He would be ready; he always was.

Standing, he then folded up his computer and began the short journey to his house.

Turning the corner, he removed the golden lighter from his pocket and began absently flipping the top open and closed, his excitement growing.

On top of my game. . . .

CHAPTER-20

Sitting at the large, rectangular table in the main conference room lined with tinted windows in the modern Miami-Dade Police Department, Manny could see the swaying palms landscaped around the building as traffic moved slowly on Second Avenue. Life was going on as usual for those people walking down the sidewalks and driving in their cars.

He sometimes wondered if people thought at all about what it took to protect them, especially from killers like Valentino. There were the gangbangers and the drug addicts and the perpetrators of domestic violence locked inside these jail walls, but he suspected most people didn't give this a second thought, especially if their lives had not been personally touched by such filth. By nature, folks were wrapped up in their own worlds, almost oblivious to anything that didn't affect them directly.

How to change that? Could it ever be changed? Yet, were law enforcement members so different from normal citizens? Workaholics knew no professional boundaries and cops thought their work more important than most. Firefighters. Military. Important, no question, but the everyday, often thankless, functions of his profession saved lives almost without appreciation.

He felt Sophie's elbow in his ribs. "Where the hell are you now, cowboy? When Swifton comes through that door, you'd better get that dreamy look out of those baby blues or she'll think you're ready for the funny farm."

"Just pondering my own narcissism."

"Does that help? You know, to get your poop in a group?"

Marie Swifton popped through the door, followed by Duane James.

"I'll let you know later," whispered Manny.

Searching the table where four other Miami-Dade detectives, two CSU supervisors, and two captains sat with Manny and the rest of the BAU, Swifton began.

"Okay, I'll get through the technical and who-has-authority-here crap then we can go on. We've invited Josh Corner and his BAU in on this one. We're after a profile, no doubt, but my experience says we'll get far more than that. What they want and what they say goes until further notice."

She hesitated, like some ghost from another case decided to streak through her mind's eye.

Manny had seen that look far more times than he cared to remember, mostly in the mirror.

Shifting in her chair, she continued. "We get our share of shit down here, but we haven't seen what they've seen. So if we don't have any questions, we'll get this meeting on the road."

One of the captains raised her hand. She was a pretty woman in her forties with blond hair and bright eyes—Penny. Penny Craig, according to her name badge.

"We've got lots of people volunteering to work overtime and help on this one, just for your information."

"That's good to know, but that'll be up to the BAU to decide if we need more or less."

Captain Craig nodded, fully understanding that too many cops involved in an investigation can hurt more than it helped sometimes.

"You all have the latest files on the four homicides in front of you. It's what we have, up until about an hour ago. And you've all seen most of what's there. We're here to listen to what the BAU has to say and then go from there. Josh?"

Josh rose out of his chair and began. "We're glad to be of any help we can. Like Marie said, this one's different in several aspects than some of the cases we have worked. With that, we're going to break this down into three aspects.

"We're going to talk about the forensic evidence, what we've found on our criminal databases, and what we're investigating. Then discuss the psychology of this killer, ending with a profile.

"I'm going to let the senior profiler conduct this meeting because frankly, he's smarter than I am, usually."

The snickers around the table told Manny that Josh had helped them relax a bit. That would be important later.

"Okay, Manny, let's do it."

Manny stood as Josh sat. "Our CSI folks are going to tell us what they've discovered and in conjunction with your own crime scene investigators, present the science."

He nodded at Dean, who still wore the teal paisley driver's hat that matched his shirt. Manny was sure Sophie's husband was getting more than one second look. If Dean noticed, he wasn't the least fazed as he began.

"You can see the time of deaths on all four victims. The first couple died some forty-four hours ago, the next two victims died right at thirty-six hours later. The first two victims died from multiple stab wounds, leading to exsanguination. The second couple died from trauma as a result of fifth-degree burns over sixty percent of their bodies."

"Why the change in method?" asked one of the four detectives.

"I'll let Special Agents Williams and Lee handle that. Right now, let's get through what we can regarding the science."

The detective nodded.

"The knives used, and left, at the first scene were nothing out of the ordinary. They were relatively expensive, but can be purchased at hundreds of stores in the Miami area. So no real leads there.

"The nylon rope used to secure the two victims to the tree is also of above-average quality, but common to the area and used on boats and ships for varying purposes. No help there either, in terms of unusual."

"A search-and-process, done by your department's CSU, showed no soil or vegetation types that were not indigenous to the area. So, we had no luck with that either."

Dean frowned and then closed his file of notes.

"Listen, I can tell you what we didn't find and go through this list of notes and scientific jargon, but we're wasting time. If you want to read this report, you can do it later. It'll probably make for a great sleep stimulate for most of you, so let me tell you what we did find."

Manny watched a couple of Miami-Dade's finest nod and grin.

"We're processing fibers that may not be from the victims' clothing. Even though he left the folks in the Everglades bound to the tree naked, it's almost impossible not to have some fibers stick to their skin if he touched them. Since he piled their clothes neatly on the backside of the tree, we can compare them with the fibers we found. If they don't belong to victims, the fibers might tell us what the perp was wearing.

"We also found a few shoe prints and footprints that we casted. This could lead to a shoe size or brand that we can compare to our databases for feet and shoes. We also have tire tracks that we'll try to match. It's a relatively secluded area but is traveled some, so those two situations may not lead to anything."

Dean ran his hand over his beard, thinking of how he wanted to present his next findings, Manny guessed. He was doing a great job in Alex's absence.

"We also located a few drops of blood spatter that appear to have fallen from the knife, but they were far from the tree. The killer could have cut himself. We'll know more when the rest of that analysis comes back from the lab.

"Again, Manny and Sophie will discuss the patterns found in the blood and the whole VALENTINO thing.

"There were no fingerprints, as anticipated with an organized killer like this one. Oh, one more thing before we get to the second crime scene. There were small, maybe fifty-cent-piece size, burn marks on the victim's ears and on the soles of their feet. To me, it looks like he used a lighter for that."

"Why a lighter?" asked Marie.

"The burns were more round, more symmetrical, and deeper burns than if he would have used a match. I say that because a match is hard to hold in one place, and the flame is at the mercy of the wind. Plus, it doesn't burn as long and has a smaller flame radius."

"God almighty. What a monster," said Penny Craig quietly.

"That's one way to put it. Let's move on to the Blanks's home," said Dean.

Hesitating, Dean glanced down at Sophie; and she put her hand on his arm. Forensic expert who'd seen some of the worst things people do to one another or not, Dean was no doubt recalling the bedroom and the evil perpetrated there. Manny knew he was.

"As I said, the Blankses died because of hypovolemia, the loss of blood and fluids to the body's extremities caused by intense exposure to heat and the decomposition of internal organs attributed to that concentrated heat."

Someone swore as Dean wavered again.

It didn't take any expert in human emotions to feel the somber mood in the room begin to morph into one of anger and loathing.

With good reason, thought Manny.

His mind once again flashed back to the man who'd raised a knife to Chloe and Ian, and he felt his own anger sharpen. For one brief moment, he pictured his hands around the killer's throat, squeezing until the son of a bitch made the journey into hell. It was what he deserved. Prison was too good for him.

Exhaling under his breath, he tore away from his thoughts of violent retaliatory justice that seemed to show up more and more lately.

Emotions didn't help any investigation, a mantra he'd preached for years. Yet, preachers weren't always right, were they? Maybe being pissed off did help focus on the purpose of catching this one, if not the punishment.

With more effort, he shook off the horrible, inhuman images of the last two days and listened as Dean continued.

"The killer used incisions to strategic areas of the bodies to cause as much internal damage as possible, and then lit the victims on fire, again on particular parts of the body using a form of accelerant—lighter fluid, we think, because of the empty can located at the scene. They were probably still alive when he finally set their bodies on fire."

Looking down to the red information file, Dean opened up to the crime scene photos taken at the Blanks's house.

"If you care to look, you can see that he used a wood-burning tool to design the virtually perfect squares in Mr. Blanks and, to a lesser extent, his mother. We don't know why he removed Mr. Blank's eyes and subsequently left his mother's intact. We haven't located the eyes as of yet, but the small stacks of ash and dust on the sofa look like organic material, so that might solve that mystery. And, before you ask, again the possible whys of all of this will be addressed during the profile session of this meeting.

"We gathered particle material here, including bagging the three tools he used to kill the Blankses. Again, no fingerprints on any of the tools or, for that matter, on the bodies. We did find one oblong, circular imprint on Gladys Blanks's ankle.

"I used to smoke as a kid, and I remember the flip lighter I had. It looks like the oval cylinder where the flame comes from, to me. We'll research that more. But if it is, that might help us to at least determine the lighter make and model. Again, not much, but it could be something.

"There were no blood traces anywhere in the house, except those on the bodies. We're not hopeful that those will lead to the killer. We have both labs, the FBI's and Miami-Dade's, working overtime to process everything we've gathered, so we hope to have more info in a few hours that could help create leads.

"There was nothing too exciting outside the house that might lead to a suspect, but we'll see."

Dean circled the table with his gaze.

"That's about all we have for now. We'll update you as soon as we have anything else. This guy just didn't make any mistakes, but science has a way of finding the smallest error in judgment. We hope that works here."

He sat down, folding his hands over the file in front of him.

Manny heard Sophie as she leaned over and whispered to her husband. "That presentation made me hot. Just saying."

For the first time today, Dean smiled. The girl knew what she was doing.

"Thanks, Special Agent Mikus. That helps, if nothing more than to show us what kind of man we're truly dealing with. Let's keep this rolling," said Marie.

Josh then nodded at Belle, and she returned his look wearing a nervous smile.

"All right. We've gone over all of our FBI databases for killing details, signatures if you will, similar to the one this killer seems to be fond of, including INTERPOL, cold case files, and any other help we can elicit.

"Thanks to your research team and a little help from Quantico, we were able to find three unsolved cases in the last twenty years that had at least partial MOs to this killer's. One in Texas, about eighteen years ago, one in Los Angles fifteen years ago, and one in Saint Kitts, about twenty years ago. All had, to varying degrees, elements that could be related to the way this man goes about his business."

Belle threw up her hands in disgust, her eyes filled with sparks. "Listen to me. I'm calling it his business instead of what it is; a perverted, psychopathic method of murder."

"You're right, Special Agent Simmons. All the more reason to get our hands on him," said Detective James.

"That's why we're here. At any rate, the two murders in the states had images carved into the bodies, and by the looks of things, both probably were killed by the same unsub. That killer didn't use initials in the forehead or have the exactness of our perp. That killer may have moved on to something else, died, or simply quit, as some serial killers do."

"I'm fairly sure, after discussing it with our staff, that we should focus our efforts on the third case in Saint Kitts."

"Why is that?" asked Marie.

"The MO fits better, for one, and the victim in Saint Kitts . . ." Belle stopped, glancing at Manny, a quick rise in pain on her face, as if begging for him to take over. He did.

"The victim in Saint Kitts was only fourteen. If that was his first victim, then he may have been around her age and thought he could control her better. If we know anything about these killers, it's that they start this type of thing early," said Manny.

"You mean the Macdonald triad theory?" asked Penny Craig.

"Sort of, although lately that combination of circumstances—bed wetting, fire starting, and animal cruelty—may not be as related as once thought. Those patterns may simply be a result of developmental behavior and related to childhood humiliation," answered Manny.

"We think if the Saint Kitts murder and these four recent deaths are related, then possibly something, some event, may have triggered the renewing of this behavior," said Belle, regaining her composure. "Just know we're going to run the full spectrum of investigation on that cold case and see what it leads to, if anything. We will get to the possible profile in a minute, but we need to share with you what's going on with the investigative side of this case.

"With the help of the city and private store owners, we're pulling every video record available that leads to and from the first crime scene. We know where the first couple lived and also where they had dinner. It may not lead to anything, but it's a shot.

"There are officers going door to door in that neighborhood, as well as the Blanks's subdivision, asking questions. We're even talking to conscrvation officers, on duty and off, at the Everglades who might have seen something or someone out of the ordinary the day of the murders or even a few days before. Given the nature of our killer's artistic tendencies, we're also contacting local art schools and colleges to see if there might be a connection that someone recognizes. Manny will talk more about what that might mean later."

Josh added, "We're also doing all of the mundane, routine investigations that don't pay off all that often, like cell phone records, credit card history, GPS locations, work profiles, and associates, as well as personal associations with friends and family. It'd be nice to find a link there."

He looked at Belle. "Thank you, Belle. I think that's about all that we have at this point. I want to give you all a few minutes to organize your thoughts, take a pee break, whatever, and we'll meet back here in ten to go over your questions and talk about possible profiles to share with your staffs."

"Before we do that, I have to ask Manny this," said Marie.

"Fire away," said Manny, suspecting what was coming.

"Belle said something about how there might be an association with the killer and Saint Kitts. Twenty years ago. Isn't that a long time for someone who is driven by a perverted, sick psychology to not express it somehow, even without a trigger event?"

Bingo. Marie had touched on the sixty-four-thousand-dollar question. Hell, it was probably worth sixty-four million.

"If there is a connection to that case—and that's a big 'if' at this point, but say there is—then we are dealing with a different kind of killer here, one who has had complete control over his impulses and motivation."

"What does that mean, exactly?" asked Detective James, standing.

Manny paused, the words forming in his mind causing him to chill.

"It means we've got a killer with a heart."

CHAPTER-21

The sun had begun its habitual, eternal fall from the purple and orange sky as she stood in front of the small window facing the west, arms folded over her breasts, contemplating the day's events and conversations.

More than ever, she was convinced that the plan, the chain of events she would begin, was right. She'd endured much. It was someone else's turn, which was inevitable. In that process, she would receive back at least a part of what she'd lost. Although fully recovering everything that had made up a promising future, even for one such as her, would take an H. G. Wells time machine to recapture.

Time.

Was there anything so unrelenting? Was any single thing more unforgiving? Did any soul go untouched by its merciless agenda?

No, none. She supposed there were people who made peace with it, even embraced the consequences of its character. But for the masses, time reminded them of their regrets and their own shortcomings as they pondered another future . . . if those regrets had been, instead, bold actions regarding their true desires.

Reaching out to the window, she touched the cool glass, leaving ghostly impressions of her fingertips.

Her smile came slowly.

She wouldn't be one of those people with regrets. She wouldn't wallow in the here and now and take life as it came her way. Not anymore.

Like those fading imprints on the glass, her future wouldn't evaporate into oblivion. Instead, it would be a bright, soaring light for her to enjoy and the world to marvel at . . . or she'd die trying.

This screwed-up rock and the path it had put her on owed her that, at the very least.

Moving to the other side of her room, the faint aroma of flowers she didn't really recognize drifting to her, she opened the closet door. She removed the suitcase from the closet, placing it gently on the bed.

As she stood straight, his face came to her again. Beautiful, handsome, full of promise, and the only one who had mattered to her from the day they met. But he, and his essence, was now out of her life in ways that no one but her could imagine.

All because of . . . them.

Fighting off the incessant, raging urge to scream, she was finally able to unclench her fists to begin packing. She had enough time.

The idea that he was gone filled her mind with a different emotion. She was now keenly aware of the excitement that revenge and justice could create and the righteousness of it.

It was almost time to set *her* desires in motion and free herself from who she'd been.

Who could ask for more?

CHAPTER-22

"How's he doing?" asked Manny.

Sophie moved away from the window of the breakroom toward Manny, stuffing the phone in her pocket.

"How is who doing?"

"Alex. You just called him, right?"

"No, I didn't," said Sophie, looking like a school kid who'd just been found guilty of some major indiscretion.

"Really?"

"Damn you, Williams. Okay. I called his butt and Barb's too. Neither answered so I left them messages, okay?"

"Okay. I was going to do it, so I'm glad you did."

"I told them both that you were using the john and you made me call."

He smiled. "I don't take that long in the restroom."

"Hey, sometimes you do. Remember that time in Cozumel, right after dinner? You were in there for, like, a year."

Manny instinctively put his hand on his stomach, recalling in great detail the evening to which she was referring.

"Good point. I don't think I'll eat escargot again any time soon."

Looking at his watch, he frowned. "He should have been out of OR by now and half coherent. Barb didn't answer either, huh?"

"Nope. I even called her twice. I figure they must have turned the phones off in case they thought you were going to bother them. Or the two of them are taking the new hand for a test run in ways I'm trying to get out of my head, you know?"

"Whoa. That's warped, even for you."

She shrugged. "You knew what you were getting when you recommended me for this gig."

"I did. I should have known better."

"Should have known better than what?" asked Josh as he and Belle approached.

"Long story," said Manny.

"It always is," said Josh.

He glanced around. "Where's Dean?"

"Vending machine break and then he said he wanted to go outside for a few minutes to clear his head," said Manny.

"I can relate," said Belle. "I'm not used to that whole public speaking arena either."

"He's a shy boy at heart for sure. Unless we're alone, then that's a different story. Did I ever tell you about the elevator in Vegas?"

"No, and you aren't going to tell them now," said Dean as he stepped to Sophie's side. "Some things are sacred."

Her smile was dazzling as she reached for Dean's hand. "Why yes, yes they are. But that doesn't mean we can't shock them with details from time to time."

"It does to me," said Manny.

"On that note, let's get this done. We've got a killer to catch and not all that much time to do it," said Josh.

Manny nodded. "Agreed. Before we do that, I have a favor to ask."

"Sure. What?"

"I'd like our folks in Quantico to chart the last two months of homicides in Miami and South Florida."

"Okay. Chart them how?"

"By the address where the body was found, cause of death, time of death, age of the victim, and home residence of the victim. Then put it in a graph format so we can check it against the city and area maps."

"Easy enough, but why?"

"It's just a hunch that'll probably be nothing."

"We know about you and your hunches. What does that mean, Williams?" asked Sophie.

"We'll talk more inside, but this guy seems to like patterns; and he's had some whacky ways to show it so far, especially considering the two hidden messages at the scenes."

"You think he started sooner than two days ago?" asked Belle.

"If it's the same guy from Saint Kitts, I'd say yes. But I'm still having a hard time reading this one," said Manny.

"Will do, then. You four get in there, and I'll be in soon." Josh walked away, phone to his ear.

Manny led the way back into the conference room and stood at the table as everyone settled in. During those few minutes, he ran through his mind everything he wanted to share. He wanted to give the locals all they needed to find this guy, but some of his ideas needed to be kept close for now. Panic on any level was still panic.

"I want to make this short and sweet," he began. "But it doesn't always end up that way."

"Whatever you think," said Marie. "We need to find this dick, and now."

"All right. This man is younger; I believe thirty-five or so. He's most certainly Caucasian. By the height of his injuries on the first two victim's bodies while bound to the tree, I'd say around five foot ten. He's fairly strong to have gotten the body of Gladys Blanks up to the fan in her room, so I'd say he's in pretty good shape.

"He's bright, well organized, as indicated by how long he takes with the victims, and has a purpose for what he's doing."

"What's that?" asked Penny Craig.

Manny ran that question around in his mind for about the millionth time. Just like all of the other instances, he couldn't get a grip on the answer.

"I'm not sure. No, that's not right. We simply don't know. He loves the display, so that indicates a certain narcissism. Yet within that display, he takes unprecedented care in finishing what he started. It could be he thinks he owes it to them, or that may suggest he has some emotional attachment to them."

"You said he has a heart, is that what you meant by your last statement?" asked Marie.

"It is. We've seen dozens of these cases, and none of those cases involved this kind of emotional commitment. I think that's where the VALENTINO reference comes from."

"You think he believes he's a great lover?" asked Duane James, frowning. "I don't follow."

"Love isn't always about the love of your life or some new boyfriend or girlfriend. It can take on a thousand faces, as we've all seen in our professional and personal lives. The cycle of domestic abuse and violence is an example.

"The abuse victim keeps coming back to the abuser because he or she knows nothing different. And, to boot, the abuser says he'll never do it again. Both are forms of love, as convoluted as that is."

Manny choose his next words carefully. "This killer loves his victims and sees himself as the greatest lover in their lives. Somehow, I believe that he thinks of himself as doing them some great, selfless favor by killing them the way he does. In his mind, he thinks he is being selfless, like all noble lovers are."

"Is it possible that he thinks he's saving them from seeing the world go deeper into the crapper?" asked Marie. "Like a savior?"

"Maybe. But I don't think he'd do what he does to the bodies if that were the case, it would probably be a bullet to the head. No suffering, no pain."

He didn't want to go too far into that line of thinking yet, so he was glad that no one had asked another question. He couldn't have answered it anyway. He didn't know why this man felt love for his victims. There was no precedent for this behavior, at least that he'd seen.

Taking a bottle of water from the table, he gathered a slow drink and continued.

"The patterns on the victims' bodies indicate his artistic ability. He's talented and seems to have the ability to make perfect shapes, even with the abnormal tools he uses. According to our sources, that's unusual in itself. As we mentioned, we've sent out several teams of blues and detectives to interview art schools, universities, and even graphic art firms for possible leads."

"But he may have never attended school around here or could be a freelancer, right?" asked one of the other detectives.

"True, but we're going with one of the best FBI theories ever. The one that says if you throw enough shit against a wall, some of it will stick."

There was ripple of laughter and a few head nods. Police work was often just that kind of trial and error.

"There is one more thing we need to discuss. It has to do with details we found at each scene that you won't see in your files. This man is very proficient in an art form called Gestalt.

"We've all seen the pictures and paintings where there is more than one image created by the artist if you look at it correctly. For instance, the picture of the old and young woman drawn from the same set of lines. Or the painting of a face that is visible if you look at the lines of a tree."

"Thanks for the art lesson, but what does that have to do with this case?" asked Duane James.

"I'll tell you. This killer used this art form to spell—in blood, by the way—'Valentino is free' at the first crime scene. He then used a wood-burning tool to do the same thing at the Blanks's home. The only difference was the message. The second one said 'And so are you.'

Another sobering silence gripped the room. Manny waited for the obvious question.

"Damn. Only in Florida. So what does that mean?" asked Penny Craig.

"On the surface, he's saying that he is free to express himself. That's not hard to gather, if we're right. The second might have to do with the victims and how they're not bound to earth anymore, but that's only a guess. It could have a deeper meaning."

"One thing it does tell us, however, is that he isn't the lover he thinks he is."

"Why?" asked Marie.

"Because the first message was about him, lending credence to the idea that he's far more about him than he realizes."

Just then, Josh walked back into the room and sat down beside Manny's chair and then motioned for him to sit.

"Excuse me," he said as he sat.

His boss leaned close and spoke softly.

"You might be on to something. I did what you asked, and the report will be on the way soon, but the tech said there is something weird with the data already."

CHAPTER-23

"Captain Swifton, we need a minute," said Manny, rising from the table. "I need to speak with my team, then we'll be back in to wrap this up."

She raised her eyebrows. "Sure. We'll be here." Once in the breakroom hall, the smell of coffee still tangoing in the air, Manny turned to Josh.

"What does 'the data is weird' mean?" asked Manny, his pulse rate climbing.

"The tech said that there were about one hundred forty homicides over the last two months, a little above normal, but nothing drastic. She said the number of shootings was down, however, but the number of others, such as knifings, beatings, and the like, were up. That caught her attention, so she then broke them down by area and how the victims were killed.

"She said the murders outside of Miami proper had spiked and had leaked into the subdivisions."

"You mean like the one where the Blankses were found," said Manny.

"Yes. But that wasn't all. It seems that there were at least three double murders that the locals have investigated that weren't shootings."

"But they wouldn't think that all unusual, given the gang and organized crime shit going on around here, right?" asked Sophie.

"Right," said Josh. "But one of them—"

Josh's phone buzzed, and he pulled it out of his pocket.

"She just sent the report with all of the graphs and maps."

"Yeah, but it's going to be hard to see and read from these phones," said Belle.

Josh turned to Dean.

"Dean. Do you still have that iPad in your briefcase?"

"I do. Hang on."

A minute later, the five of them huddled around the eight-inch screen as Josh sent the report.

Dean opened the email and then pressed the PDF file logo. A few moments later, six graphs and three charted maps, stacked three by three, covered the screen.

This is only the first batch, read the title of the email.

"What were you going to say?" asked Manny, looking at Josh.

"I was going to say that there were two female employees of a local computer store found bludgeoned to death in a park on the outskirts of the city. The first report said they were robbed and then killed with a hammer as they lay on their backs."

Manny saw Sophie flinch. He wondered briefly why he hadn't. He'd have to worry about that later. They were getting close to something here.

He thought about what he'd requested from the lab, the knowledge of the older double murder adding fuel to those ideas.

Shapes and their meanings were important to this man. He may not even realize how important. Had he subconsciously screwed up? Manny's emotions did the roller-coaster ride again as his excitement stirred.

Tapping the screen, he asked Dean a question. "So did the tech send a map plotting out the double murders over the last two months?"

"Let's find out. If not, she can whip one up in a hurry."

The first map wasn't the right one. It displayed all of the murders, double homicides and others, outside of Miami proper, with color-coded dots connected by numerous lines.

Working expertly, Dean opened the second.

It revealed a much smaller nebulous pattern of dots and lines that were much clearer than the first map.

"This isn't it either," said Dean. "This is all of the murders that were committed without a gun, single and double homicides."

"Next," said Manny.

A moment later, the map flowered on the screen, and instantly Manny knew what they were looking at was his theory in practice.

There were three dots, connected by two lines, giving the impression of the top three sides of a perfect diamond. The pattern started where the two women from the computer store were found, then moved north and west to the Everglades to the tree where the young couple was killed. Then, beginning from the top of the diamond again, the line stopped at where he guessed was the Blanks's home in the subdivision east and north of the crime scene for the two computer store employees.

Manny again touched the screen.

"This is it, isn't it? What you were thinking?" said Sophie.

"I think so. He's so obsessed with his art, his passion, and his love affair with patterns, that he may not have realized what he was doing. But, then again, he may have."

"You mean, to taunt us?' asked Belle.

"I don't think he's the taunting type. He may just be compelled to show his genius. There's a difference between those two ideas for men like him. I'm just not sure yet. But if we do this right, we just might find out."

Pointing to the screen again, Manny touched the bottom of the diamond that, as yet, had no dot or lines running to it to complete the shape.

"Dean, how far is it from the top point to the sides of this pattern?"

Pulling the inch-equals-a-mile scale from the bottom of the map, Dean superimposed the lines from the top dot to the two side dots, extending them until they intersected at one point.

Dean shook his head. "That can't be right," he said. Then he repeated the action.

Glancing up at Manny, he shrugged.

"This is nuts. According to this, the distance from the top dots to the side dots is exactly six point five miles for both of them. I mean *exactly*."

"It makes sense, in a twisted, serial-killer sort of way," said Manny.

"Now let's make an intersecting point from the side dots to the bottom of the diamond directly below the top dot, exactly six and a half miles away."

Dean hit the keys on the pad's screen with gusto, completing the perfectly-shaped diamond with a fourth dot. He then magnified the screen until an address displayed.

"This says the property belongs to Grayson Pool Company. It seems to be a warehouse where they keep their supplies," said Dean.

"Is that it? Is that where he kills again?" asked Sophie.

"I think so," said Manny softly.

"How did you know?" asked Josh.

"I didn't until we got the info on the last double murder, which looks like it was his work as well, without the engraved circles or burnt squares. I was only thinking about what he's obsessed with, at least part of it. I still don't know why he's doing what he's doing. "

"Can we do something else here?" asked Belle.

"Sure, what?"

"If his pattern stays true, he'll kill again in under twenty-eight hours. But can we get the time of death from those poor ladies that were beaten?"

"Sure," answered Dean.

Manny felt his unease grow as Dean searched.

"According to the ME's report, it was four days, almost to the hour before the second double murder at the tree."

"So that means he reduced his time from the first to the second and to the third murders about twelve hours, again, assuming that first incident is his. So what's to say he won't change it again?" said Belle.

Manny exhaled. "That's great thinking, Belle. There's nothing that says he won't because we don't know where he's coming from, totally."

"Say he does change his agenda. It would most likely be in twelve-hour increments, by my calculation," said Josh.

"So our best guess is twelve hours, or will he really go twenty-four?" asked Sophie.

"Belle? What do you think?' asked Manny.

"Well, if he stays consistent, I'd say twelve hours, leaving him in the middle of his established design. But his agenda is his own, so anything is possible," she said.

"Even if he moves his schedule up to kill again in twelve hours, we still have time," said Manny.

Josh stepped toward the conference room. "All right. I'll go talk to Marie and her crew, and we'll get people out to this address."

"Wait. You have to make sure she does that discreetly. We don't know if he's planning to take his next victims there, or if they work there or own the place. Also, we can assume by the nature of the target building, he's likely to use water somehow for these next murders. We need to give her that information."

"Water? Makes sense. But what should they watch out for?" asked Josh.

"I'm not that well versed on what goes on around here. Hell, I don't know. The beaches. Clubs with pools. Maybe even pools where these people have done work. Maybe the fire department or the life guards association can help. That should be her call," said Manny.

Pausing, Manny listened even closer to his instincts. "You know, if he does accelerate to the whole twelve hours, that only leaves four left. He'll also want some prep time, depending what's next."

"So?" asked Sophie.

"We need to go out there now," said Manny. "At the worst, we can have the owners meet us there to see if they've seen anyone or anything out of the ordinary over the last few days. Best case, we catch his ass."

"Pretty optimistic, aren't we?" asked Josh.

"Maybe, but I think we've got a bead on his next round of fun. That might mean we end all of this."

"Good idea. I want you to wait until I can get a couple of squad cars to go with you," said Josh.

"We need to go now. Besides, we're still cops and we'll have Sophie, stars and all," said Manny.

"Bet your ass," said Sophie.

"You're sure?"

"Yes. You can have some blues in the neighborhood if you want, but I'd rather it just be us. We can be in and out before dinner."

"Have it your way, but be careful. All right. You four head out there now, and I'll brief Marie. She can send a unit or two, like you asked, to watch the area. Make sure you call so we know what's going on."

Manny nodded. But there was another situation that had been playing on his mind, especially if this killer took only twelve hours away from his schedule, providing he took any at all; there was time to nail two birds with one stone.

"I think Dean, Sophie, and I can handle it. I'd like you two to do something else, if you're willing."

"Damn. That's always trouble when you ask something like that. But fire away," said Josh.

"I'd like you to fly to Saint Kitts and talk to the local police department."

His eyes shifted to Belle. She stiffened but stayed silent.

"Why?" asked Josh.

"It's a small island, and they can't have had a lot of crime over the years, unless I miss my guess. The murder of Belle's friend had to be big news. Such an experience had to be shocking and unusual. There might be things to learn that no database of cold cases will discover."

Looking at Belle, Josh raised his hands. "That makes sense to me, but that's probably a two-hour flight down and another two hours back. You might need us."

"True, but I think Marie's people can handle the muscle side. There isn't much profiling or analytical work to do now. It's a good time for you to skip down there."

"Not to mention, I'll have the opportunity to face the thing that still gives me nightmares, right?" said Belle, stone faced.

"If that comes up, then yes. I was thinking more of how you still remember the details of Cammy's murder and that they can't pull a fast one on you, if they try."

"That's a good point too," said Josh.

Belle twisted her head, her neck cracking. "You think they might be hiding something?"

Manny shrugged. "I only think that it's a small island, and I wonder how many white kids that age were living or vacationing there at that time, among other things. Plus, I know you have a few questions of your own."

Josh nodded. "Okay. We'll go. Maybe we can get a name or something. You head to the warehouse and stay in contact with Marie and don't do anything stupid."

With that, he headed toward the conference room.

Belle tilted her head toward Manny, a thin smile crossing her mouth. "If I go crazy, you'll be the first to know."

"Then you'll be part of the club," said Sophie. "We're all damn nuts."

"Hard to argue with that," she answered, then followed Josh.

"Let's get our butts in gear. Timing is everything, and we just might find what we're looking for," said Manny.

"I hope so. Maybe we can stay here a couple of extra days for a little sun," said Dean as they walked to the elevator.

"That would work. I can work on my thong lines," said Sophie.

"One can only hope," said Manny.

"What does that mean?" she asked.

"Nothing. I just hope you're right about getting to work on your thong lines."

They reached the black SUV parked on the street near the front of the building.

Sophie got in the driver's side, complained about the heat, and then quickly started the truck. She revved it up a couple of times, grinning like the Mad Hatter. Then his partner slammed it into drive and pulled away from the curb.

The three of them talked about nothing and everything for the twenty minutes it took them to get to Grayson's Pool Company, something they seldom did these days.

It was intentional, in Manny's eyes. There was only so much cop shit any of them could take in a day. That *anyone* could take in a day.

Reaching the white building with teal and orange lettering, based on the Miami Dolphins football team, they pulled into the side parking lot and got out.

The evening sun had sunk beneath the horizon as darkness rapidly approached.

"I think we missed them. It looks like this place is closed," said Dean.

"Maybe Grayson and his son haven't gotten here yet," said Manny.

"Or that."

They approached the glass door on the front of the building, and Manny immediately saw that the lights had been turned off.

He checked the door. Locked.

Turning to Dean and Sophie, he pulled his phone from his pocket.

"I'll call them again."

As he hit the recall button, he caught sudden movement out of the corner of his eye.

Spinning toward the glass door, his adrenaline spiking high, he watched through the semi-light as a man dropped to the floor and then disappeared from his sight.

CHAPTER·24

The FBI's Gulfstream banked a few degrees left as Belle felt it level off. It had been only forty-five minutes since they left the police department's conference room, but rank had its privileges and getting a federal jet in the air was a small task for Josh to pull off.

What her new boss lacked in investigative skills—though he was above average in that department—he made up for with how he handled the administrative part of his job. No one could have gotten them in the air faster. She wasn't sure that was such a blessing, however.

She studied him as he talked on the phone and, when he abruptly hung up, catching her stare, she didn't glance away.

"Do I have something on my face?" he asked.

"No, well, yes, but you can't help it."

"That means what?"

"It means you aren't only a good-looking boss man, but you are the perfect fit to lead this BAU."

"Have you been talking to Sophie, or are you trying to suck up and get me to turn this jet around?"

"I'll confess to both. You caught me. Will it work?"

"Nope. Nice try, though. We might have something here with your friend's case and Valentino being related."

Belle nodded, fighting the twisting aerobics the butterflies were performing in her stomach. Manny and Josh were right. There could be a break in the case by going to Saint Kitts. But neither of them had known it as long as she had, whatever that meant in the great scheme of things. She had never been good with confrontation, but she'd have to be tonight.

In about an hour and a half, she and Josh would talk to the inspector who had led Cammy's murder investigation as well as the head of the island's police department to see what they could uncover. It didn't matter what she really wanted to do, which was to hide her head until this whole thing was over. But that was part of this world of cops and crooks, wasn't it?

You don't always get what you want.

"You hanging in there?" asked Josh.

"Yes. I'll be fine. I hope the others won't need us, that's all."

"We gave the Miami-Dade people all they needed. Let's hope that's enough."

"It will have to be. Besides Manny, Sophie, and Dean will be there to help keep them together. And I think we have time before the perp cranks it up again," said Belle, trying to get her mind away from the upcoming meeting.

"Do you really think we do? That he's not going kill again for another sixteen hours?"

Belle crossed her legs. Did she? She was a profiler first and foremost. She wasn't Manny, but she thought she had a bead on this unsub.

"Yes. I think we do. I just can't see him breaking with the symmetry he's established, as far as we can see it."

"Good. That'd how I see it too."

Josh got up and moved into the chair directly in front of her, leaning forward as he spoke.

"Listen. I know this will be tough for you. I also suspect you knew this was coming the second you shared your experience on Saint Kitts. But, as I've learned working with one Special Agent Manny Williams for a few years, there are times to face and slay the dragon. We just have to remember we aren't doing it alone."

"Some dragons are meaner than others."

"Yeah, still only a dragon, though. I'll be right there, and I know you. You're a tough woman, even though you like jazz."

Even she enjoyed the laugh that escaped from not just her lips, but her heart.

"Jazz is God's music and don't forget it."

Josh bowed his head reverently, smiling.

"Yes ma'am. I'll remember that."

Belle felt her load lighten some.

Kids carry burdens well into their adult lives, even to their graves, most of the time not understanding why. She'd understood this one perfectly. In fact, it had been a driving force for her to become a cop.

Yet, to hear Josh talk about facing this stress alongside her had been far more comforting than any pep talk or determined rationale she'd bestowed upon herself over the last twenty years.

Safety in numbers, she supposed. And the man was good looking, for what that was worth. Good looking—and married.

She shook off where her mind was heading with that line of thinking and stood.

"I'll buy you a cup of coffee, and we can talk more about how we want to handle this meeting."

"That's a good idea. These two are going to be defensive, I'd guess, but we have to get through all of that and find out what they know."

Balancing two cups of hazelnut cream coffee, she returned to her seat and handed one to Josh.

"I've been thinking about that," she said. "About our approach."

"And?"

"We have to start slowly, small talk, then tell them about the murders in South Florida. Then talk about Cammy's murder and how they might be related. When they begin the stonewalling of information we know they have, we drop the bomb on them that I'm the American girl who saw the killer. When we do that, we'll have to watch them closely."

"What will I be watching for?" asked Josh, a gleam in those blue eyes.

"Their eyes and expressions will take up the next part of this interview," she said.

"Which will be what?"

Sipping her coffee, Belle looked at her knee. Without raising her eyes to Josh, she told him.

"The identity of Cammy's killer."

CHAPTER-25

"Sophie and Dean, stay here and guard the front door, I'm heading toward the back."

"Why?" said Sophie, dropping Dean's hand.

"There's someone inside, and I don't think it's the cleaning lady."

"It could be an employee," said Dean.

"No cars in the lot and the Graysons said they'd meet us here because they were closed for the day," said Manny.

"Watch your ass, Williams. We've got this," said Sophie, pulling her weapon with one hand, two pink throwing stars with the other.

Manny sprinted around the side of the building, making a mental note of the two shipping docks equipped with fifteen-foot doors on the side of the building. They could be escape routes, but the dim red lights above them indicated they were locked and would be far too noisy and cumbersome to use for an escape.

Steps later, he turned the corner of the building and came to rest in front of the rust-streaked metal double doors that should have been locked.

The left one was slightly ajar, showing only darkness as he strained for any semblance of light.

He switched his Glock to his right hand and slowly climbed the pitted cement steps.

Once he reached the doors, he stopped, trying to get a glimpse of light through the pitch black of the slivered opening.

Reaching for the door with his left hand, he pushed it open an inch at a time, his bundled nerves on complete alert as the perspiration formed in uniform dots across his forehead. And it wasn't because of the heat.

The warm, dusty warehouse odor invaded his heightened sense of smell, causing him to pause yet again until he detected nothing out of the ordinary. He felt no need to run into a burning warehouse trap.

After making sure that he was not, he moved forward.

He hated this part of police work. Walking into the devil's dark playhouse was the one thing that made him take pause. Many a good cop had been sent to their funerals in situations like this, and he had no intentions of adding to that number.

I'm getting too old for this shit.

With that thought vivid in his mind, he moved cautiously, opening the door even further.

Sophie and Dean were good—they had each other up front—but maybe he should call for backup. It was the safest thing and was in line with proper police procedure. But what he didn't know was how many ways there were to leave this building undetected. Backup would probably be too late to help cover that anyway.

If this man inside was Valentino, and they had timed their arrival just right, who was he to fly in the face of providence?

His hyper-sense went into overdrive, without the trance state Sophie and Alex often chided him about.

The man who had ducked out of sight in the front of the building *was* Valentino. There was no question in his mind. They had done good police work and solved his puzzle, intentional or subconscious as it was, and maybe now they could reap those rewards.

Taking one step closer to the completely opened, but still dark doorway, Manny saw a dim aura of light to the right of the door's breach radiating from safety lights somewhere near the west end of the building. They revealed a flight of four concrete steps leading to the main floor of the building.

His gun held ready, he slid through the door, crouching low, then quickly reached against the wall, his fingers desperately seeking a light switch.

Just as his hand touched the cool metal plate leading to the light switches, he heard a familiar sound. The plate exploded.

He fell back against the side of the steps, hidden from the source of the shot, the passing pain in his fingers and the thumping in his chest reminding him that he wasn't bulletproof.

The unsub had shot out the light plate with a weapon fitted with a suppresser. He had to be fairly close for Manny to hear the muffled report and for the shooter to be fairly accurate—unless, of course, he was also an expert marksman. In that case, Manny's ass was grass and the shooter was the lawn mower.

"This is the FBI, asshole, drop your weapon and you might get out of here alive," he yelled.

The response was so quick it surprised Manny.

"Asshole? Is that any way to speak to greatness, Agent Williams?"

There was no ignoring the bone-shaking chill that touched every corner of his being. This man was supremely confident and had somehow been expecting them.

Regaining his composure, no small feat this time, he answered back, hoping to piss off his adversary.

"You're a killer, Valentino. That's not greatness; that's being a coward."

"You are a charmer, aren't you? You also have no concept of what I've done."

His voice wasn't far away, but the echo from within the warehouse proved too muddled to get a true bead on his location. Touching his phone, he wanted to text Sophie, but then stopped; the light from the face of the cell could alert Valentino of his intention. He stuck with trying to get the lunatic off his game.

"You murdering six people isn't a concept, you sick bitch. It's a crime."

"Not a crime for me, Agent. I did them a favor because I loved them. I gave them what everyone secretly desires."

The location of Valentino's voice told Manny that he was in the same general position or close to it.

"An early funeral after you tortured them? You didn't have that right."

"No, not an early funeral, Agent, and certainly not torture. In the end, they all understood. I gave them something far more eternal, more tangible than a few more years of life."

"Yeah, what was that?"

The killer was so calm, so sure of himself. Manny's uneasiness grew with his awareness that there had to be something else happening with this man . . . and this meeting.

"Are you going to answer me, dickhead?"

"Yes, even though you are acting like a ten-year-old with the name calling. That's okay, however. I forgive you."

His location had changed slightly, but Manny was still in the lurch as to where. Damn it.

He'd been gone longer than he should have. Sophie would know what that meant and had probably called for backup by now.

Keep him talking, Williams.

"Spare me your indignation and forgiveness. I don't give a rat's ass."

"Suit yourself. But let me answer your question before I go. I gave them fame, Agent. I gave them a true immortality. They will forever be remembered because my talent and love made it so. No one else could give them what I have. No one."

This time the voice was farther away.

Shit.

"Where are you going? We have more to discuss. Like how your new boyfriend likes it when you get to prison."

"Goodbye, Agent. I only wanted to introduce myself to the best of the best at what you do so you could know that I am the best at what I do. I—"

The large overhead lights suddenly flooded the building, causing him to squint with purpose.

"Just shut the hell up and drop your weapon."

Sophie.

There was another muffled shot, then a second, followed by two quick shots as Sophie fired back.

Rising from his spot, his eyes almost focused, Manny ran up the three steps then hit the floor, rolling toward a pallet of boxes, as more gunfire echoed through the building.

"Sophie! You okay?"

The silence that followed caused his stomach to drop to his feet.

Maybe she didn't want to give her position away.

"Yeah. It'll take more than this creep to send me packing," she finally answered.

He'd never heard anything so sweet in his life.

Another bullet ripped into the boxes directly above his head and he went closer to the floor.

A second later, he heard Sophie swear.

She fired off three more quick shots from his left. He then reached around the corner of the pallet, sure of Sophie's location, and fired twice in the general direction from where Valentino last fired.

Immediately after, he thought he heard a groan of pain, then the boxes above him rained porcelain and cardboard on his head and back.

"Williams?" yelled Sophie.

"Still breathing."

"I think he's hit," she said. "Maybe he's dead."

Manny prayed she was right as the silent lull in the clamor of gunfire stole over the building. It only lasted for an instant.

The next sound that rattled throughout the warehouse was the slamming of a heavy door.

Valentino had left the building.

CHAPTER-26

Scrambling to his feet, Manny met Sophie in the middle of the warehouse floor.

"Did you see which way he went?" asked Sophie.

"No. But it had to be in that corner," he said, pointing toward the area of the building where he'd fired.

They hurried in that direction reaching a slight bend where a stack of pallets stuck out over the yellow walking path.

Holding up his hand, Manny motioned for Sophie to stop. They then moved slowly, finally peeking around the corner, Sophie low, Manny high.

"Shit," she said.

Down another flight of stairs, angled away from them, the side emergency exit door stood wide open.

They could see the last embers of the Florida sunset blending with the now fully lit security lights through the opening, but no Valentino.

Sophie hurried to get in front of Manny and then abruptly stopped, squatting on her haunches, staring at the floor.

"What is it?"

"Blood, Big Boy. One of us hit him, and there is more of it through the door."

She stood and then hopped down the steps, halfway out into the warm Miami night.

Manny called to her. "Wait."

She turned toward him. "What? The prick's not out there waiting for us. Especially since backup will be here any second. He's running his nuts off, if he has any. We have to track his ugly ass down."

Manny scanned the warehouse. "How did you get in here? I told you to stay put."

"Hey, I have a skill or two. That front door lock was nothing. We can talk about how I saved your ass later. Let's go."

"I said hold up. Where's Dean?" he asked.

"He's out front in the SUV waiting for backup . . . oh no."

Manny's and Sophie's relationship stretched back almost fifteen years together, and he thought he'd seen every imaginable expression from her, but the absolute panic etched on her pretty face at that moment was a first.

For the umpteenth time this trip, his worry meter hit the roof. His heart felt as if it was on a proverbial yoyo.

Reacting like a scared cat, Sophie tore up the steps and past him, sprinting with the determination of an Olympian.

He fell in line behind her, trying to keep up as she wound her way through the aisles and toward the front door she'd managed, somehow, to open.

It was impossible to not link their mad dash with so many others they'd taken part in over the years, including the one where he caught the man who had threatened Ian and Chloe. He hoped this would turn out better than most of the rest of them.

Reaching the front door, Sophie burst through, flew down the steps, and turned to the side parking lot where they'd parked the SUV.

Manny reached her side just as the high beams, accompanied by the roaring engine, told them the SUV was intent on making road kill out of both of them.

Reacting on instinct alone, he grasped her shoulder, pulling her tight, and yanked her away from the oncoming vehicle, hitting the hard surface with far more impact than he'd intended.

They rolled over on the uneven concrete two times, barely avoiding the SUV's reckless charge. Sophie yelped once, and Manny fought to capture lost breath. But they were alive, at least for the moment.

Sophie broke free from him, dazed but determined, as they both scrambled to their feet just in time to see the taillights of the SUV disappear away from the driveway, motoring left on the side street.

"You son of a bitch," screamed Sophie.

"We need to look for him, Sophie. Maybe he's not in the vehicle," said Manny.

They went up and down the exterior of the building and then searched through the row of palms bordering the property. After one more desperate sweep of the building, Manny met Sophie where Valentino had almost taken them out.

The look on Sophie's face at the moment was far worse than the one in the warehouse a few minutes earlier.

There was no Dean Mikus in sight.

CHAPTER-27

"You're so beautiful. You look like an angel. You are one, aren't you?"

Barb smiled, despite the turmoil running rampant in her soul.

"No, Alex. We've been through this twice. I'm your wife Barbara, and we're in the hospital after surgery to give you a new hand, remember? You're still under the effects of the anesthetic and pain medication."

His eyes grew wide. "What? A new hand? What was wrong with the other one?"

"You didn't have one. You lost it in San Juan almost two years ago."

"Well, I'm no expert, but how in God's name does one lose a hand? I mean, they're on pretty tight, aren't they?"

She laughed out loud.

"Yes, Alex, they are on pretty tight. There was sword play involved and—"

"That crazy bastard Caleb Corner whacked it off. Yeah, I remember, vividly," he finished.

Barb rose from her chair and kissed him on the lips, then pinched his cheek hard enough for him to squint with pain.

"You are a bad boy for tricking mama. I'm going to have to punish you," she said, adding a touch of sexy to her voice.

"Oh boy. But I think you're going to have to wait for a few days. They said no sudden movements or thrashing around for a while. And that hurt."

"It was supposed to. That's what you get for being deceitful. And I have other ways, Alexander Downs, of inflicting a little damage. You won't see me coming until it's too late."

"That would be too bad. I like to see you coming," he said, grinning.

"Why, yes you do, so you won't get to see it."

"I lose."

Taking a step back, she looked at his left arm again. It was fully immobilized by a series of straps and metal belts that ran all of the way up to his shoulder. They were intended to keep the thinly spiked contraption that looked like it had escaped from a Gene Roddenberry movie from moving even a millimeter.

Over one hundred pins stuck into the surface of Alex's flesh just around where the prosthetic had been surgical fused with his lower arm. There must have been twice that many spiraling up to his shoulder.

She thought this contrivance represented the full range of what was good and bad in the marriage of contemporary technology and medicine. If it did the trick, great. If it didn't; what was the price for failure? On top of all of that, her husband was going to be laid up for far more than a few days.

That little tidbit was going to prove to be a problem and a relief simultaneously when the time came, but she'd handle it like always.

"Quite a contraption, isn't it? Some of it is overkill to ensure nothing moves, but better to be safe than sorry."

"That's true. Are you in any pain, Alex?"

He shook his head. "I can't feel anything with the arm. The pins are to help keep the impulse connectors in place, but they also act a little like needles from an acupuncture treatment by shutting down certain other nerve endings. I understand the science in principle, but not the specifics in the process," he said, that geek expression that he and Dean held dear coming into play.

"Well, you don't have to understand everything."

"No, but it's nice to have a clue."

"If you say so. Oh, by the way, Sophie, Dean, Manny, and Josh all called and left messages on both our phones. They want to know how you're doing. Sophie wanted to know if you and I had tried out the new hand yet."

His eyes were alive, even as he shook his head in a disapproving way.

"That girl only has two things on her mind. Sex and giving me a hard time."

"Yep."

"I appreciate the love, from all of them, though. I'll call them tomorrow and give them an update after I talk to the docs."

"That sounds like a plan, but I don't think you'll be talking to these doctors tonight or tomorrow even."

"What the hell does that mean?"

She stuck the hypodermic needle into his right arm and watched as he went out almost immediately.

Stroking the side of his face with her hand, she spoke softly.

"I have other plans for you, Alex Downs."

CHAPTER-28

The first Miami-Dade police cruiser rolled around the corner and slammed to a stop in front of the stoop of the building.

"About damned time," said Sophie, hurrying to the car.

Manny put his phone back in his pocket after dialing Marie Swifton but not giving the cell time to connect.

He high-stepped it to Sophie's side.

She broke off to the right, not looking in his direction, swung around the driver's side, yanked opened the door, and pulled the driver out of the car.

"Hey, what are you doing?" said the pudgy driver.

"I called you guys twelve minutes ago, and you're just getting here now. By the looks of things, you must have stopped and had another damned doughnut. If I had time, I'd kick your asses."

"Easy, Sophie," said Manny, already heading for the passenger's seat.

"Easy my homesick ass, Manny."

She turned back to the driver.

"Just get the hell out of the way. I need this car."

"I can't let you—"

With one lightening flick of her hand, she put the officer on his knees.

"I'll take whatever the hell I want. You can bill the FBI."

She jumped in behind the wheel, just as the cop's partner jumped out, allowing Manny to climb in.

"It's been five minutes since he left. He could be anywhere," said Manny.

"Just strap up and let me worry about that," she said.

He did.

Sophie spun the green-and-white around in a semicircle, working the accelerator and brakes, the acrid aroma of burning rubber surging through the cruiser, and then sped out of the parking lot.

"Good move," he said, watching her closely.

"I have better ones. I'll show you later."

She was upset, as anyone would be, but she was with him.

"So you have a way to track his phone with GPS?" asked Manny.

"I do, sort of."

She ran a stop sign at the next intersection, causing Manny to flinch, and then stepped on the accelerator. She then reached into her pocket and threw him her phone.

"I know this ain't up your alley, but there's an icon on my phone that has a tiny picture of Dean's head. He's wearing that freaking ugly yellow paisley hat. Press that."

The phone flashed and suddenly a grid map of streets, which Manny assumed were in this section of Miami, appeared. Almost instantly, he saw the red blinking light toward the upper left corner of her phone. The steady green light was on the opposite side.

"Are there three lights?"

"Yes, red, amber, and green. The red and amber are almost on top of each other. I'm assuming we're the green light?"

Her relief was almost palatable, to say nothing of his own. They'd located Dean.

His partner wiped at her eyes, swinging around a car parked illegally on the road, not missing a beat.

"Yes. The amber is Dean, and the red is his phone."

"What does that mean?" asked Manny.

"It means that after the crazy shit that went down in Vegas, we are always going to know where each of us is. We both had GPS chips embedded in our calves to make sure of it. Now, touch the red button."

"Good idea," he said, touching the red light.

A white banner with an address scrolled over the screen, the number on the address changing as the scrolling continued.

"Can you read it, Manny? Do you know where the SUV is? Is it moving or did it stop?"

"Yes. Yes. Yes, it's moving, to answer your questions. In about one block, you'll reach Parker Street, and then go right."

"Good answers. Again, I underestimated you with technology," she said.

"Hey, I don't like it that much, but it works. It's like broccoli. I don't like that either, but I eat it."

"Yeah, I'm like that with liver," she answered, her voice stronger.

Sophie had steeled herself. Her tears had dried, and her demeanor had become focused on her task—finding Dean and keeping him safe. She'd come a long way in that area of her professional life, yet he heard it anyway, that underlying fear-driven tone that maybe she wouldn't be able to keep Dean away from pain or, worse, that Valentino was going to take away the only truly good thing in her life.

He knew where she was coming from. There has never been a more diabolical idea contrived in the almost limitless thoughts of humans than one that conveys true helplessness. We all feel it at some point. New mothers to old grandfathers. New lovers to old lovers. All are far too familiar with that heartache.

The terrible emotional hybrid of anger and worry began to rise up in the middle of his chest at the thought of what Sophie must be going through.

Spinning the steering wheel, Sophie screamed onto Parker and stomped the gas.

"Where next?" she said.

"In four blocks, turn west on Bird Road. It looks like he's heading away from the city."

"How about those lights on my phone?"

"If you mean are both of Dean's indicator lights still together and lit, yes."

"Thank you."

She licked her lips then glanced at him.

"I hate this son of a bitch. He scares me," she said.

"We got this. Don't worry. He's just another psycho."

But that wasn't true, was it?

He wanted to share with Sophie what Valentino had said about his inspiration. His mission of making people famous was unlike any other motivation for a serial killer he'd yet seen or even read about. He kept it to himself.

There would be time for that discussion later.

Valentino's cool, calm voice played over in his head, enticing thoughts that were almost unfamiliar to him. He thought about the scumbag, and men like him, who had threatened his family.

Manny squeezed Sophie's phone tighter.

Justice had always been at the top of his list of priorities. Part of his mantra included the idea that everyone accused of a crime deserved a fair shake, but he wondered if his approach had been littered with ideals that only applied to fools, especially for killing machines like this asshole.

At this moment, living in Sophie's torture with her, the only justice he was interested in had to do with the spilling of Valentino's blood. For once, he chose to entertain that notion as truth.

*****

Watching the man behind the wheel of the SUV, his free hand pointing the Berretta at his face, Dean wondered how someone so ordinary in appearance had evolved into something so extraordinarily appalling. But that would be like asking why the world spun west to east instead of the other way around.

It was just how it was.

He felt his on-again/off-again compulsion, brought to the forefront during stress like this, to rid himself of germs, screaming at him to wring his hands together and eliminate the source of that compulsion. But he resisted, for now.

Sophie had helped him work through that his germ phobias, and he didn't want to backtrack if he could help it. He was more confident in himself than ever before, yet even that had its limits. But what choice did he have? He knew if he didn't get out of this vehicle soon it could be too late.

"Why don't you let me go? What am I to you? Besides, you'll be able to move faster."

Valentino kept his eyes on the road as he spoke.

"We're moving just fine, Agent. And while your logic is sound, and I don't really need you, you might be more important to me than you believe. Plus, there's another consideration to make here."

His captor slowed for the next intersection, turned left, wincing as he did.

Dean guessed by the exchange of gunfire in the warehouse and the small blot of blood at the right shoulder, Valentino had been hit by Sophie or Manny.

"You should get that looked at. It could be worse than you believe."

"Thank you for your concern, Agent. But I'll be fine. I've had worse injuries without treatment."

"All right then, but infection is always a possibility."

No response.

Dean felt his pulse quicken as he asked his next question.

"What do you mean another consideration? You mean because I've seen your face?"

"Yes, that's what I mean."

He followed that with a quick, almost pleasant smile as he glanced at Dean.

The terrible compulsion to tear the skin from his body rose to another level. He slowly began to rub his thumb against his other hand.

"It'll be only a matter of time before we know who you are anyway."

"How so?" Valentino's tone gave away no perceptible concern.

"You've left a surprising amount of DNA behind, assuming you were bleeding in the warehouse as well. Fingerprints and facial recognition software can be used from the security cameras at the—"

His hands began to work harder against each other as realization grabbed him by the front of his paisley shirt.

"You know all of this, don't you? You're doing this, broadcasting your identity, on purpose."

*****

"Left. Go left on the next road."

"Hold on."

Manny braced himself against the dash as the car picked up speed. At the right second, Sophie slammed on the brakes, burning more rubber, causing the vehicle to fishtail to the left. As it swung back right, she gunned it, and the car straightened onto the road where Manny had instructed her to turn.

"You should get a job driving for a NASCAR team."

"I will. I swear it. Right as soon as I get Dean away from that murdering piece of shit and then stuff a couple of my stars up Valentino's ass for good measure."

Usually Manny would laugh, and ordinarily she'd mean for him to do just that, but not this time.

She was serious. And he believed on all accounts.

"How far away is that SUV now?"

"It looks like less than a mile. They're still on this road."

The cruiser picked up speed.

"We're almost there, and I don't think he has any idea we're after him. He couldn't have. We'll get him back, Sophie."

"I know we will. That's not what's scaring the living crap out of me."

"What then?"

She looked at him, and even in the dim light radiating from the instrument panel, he could see the anguish on her face.

"I know I'll see him again. I just want him to be breathing."

*****

"How perceptive of you, Agent. It is good to know that the FBI has some intellectual ability after all."

With all of the strength he could muster, Dean separated his hands and rested one on each thigh. He felt like some high-powered electromagnet was pulling at him, but he held steady, for now.

"I'd say that we do. But why are you doing this, exposing yourself? It can only end badly for you."

Valentino shifted the gun closer to his lap. It was still pointed directly at Dean, but it didn't seem as menacing.

Maybe, just maybe . . .

"You've no doubt heard that people and their skills and talents are seldom appreciated in their hometowns, for whatever reason, yes?"

"I have. So you feel underappreciated? For what? Killing innocent people?"

Dean could see him gather his thoughts, obviously battling to control himself, upset over Dean's statement.

"No. Let me explain it to you like I did Agent Williams. And yes, I did my research. I know who you all are. But you miss the point. That's not it at all. I'm not murdering these people like you morons believe. I'm using my talents to immortalize them. To make them famous and help them leave a legacy that they wouldn't have without me. I love them. I want only good things for them."

Resisting bringing his hands together, Dean reached to stroke his beard.

"Easy agent. Keep your hands on your lap."

He complied, but his mind traveled the same trail. Crazy spiced with delusional didn't come close to describing this man.

"You love them? Yet you kill them like that?"

"I don't expect you to understand, but years and years down the road, they will be remembered."

"As will you, right?"

"That wasn't my intent, to begin with. But genius must be shared. The best of the best, and their work, their creations, must be given to the masses."

"So by exposing the world to your 'creations' you're killing two birds with one stone? You know there is no way in hell those crime scene photos will ever be made public. It won't happen."

He felt the vehicle begin to slow down.

"Do you know that one of those talentless cops called me a sick son of a bitch?" There was more tension in the man's voice. "Sick. We'll see about that. What I have in mind is far better than exposure, Agent. I'm going to let the public decide what is true art, true love, true genius. Not warped or demented actions of a madman, but quite the opposite."

Dean's heart sank. "The Internet? You're going to post pictures of those two crime scenes?"

His grin was clearly visible as the SUV slowed even more.

"Not two creations, Agent, but four, to begin with. You've seen only two. The third one is awaiting discovery. Perhaps my gallery will help hasten that discovery."

"You've killed eight people?"

"Not exactly. I believe the two women I shot out of necessity don't really matter in the grand scheme of what is happening here. And the first four, from my youth . . . well, they don't really count either. There is one more gallery up for review along with the Welches and the Blankses . . . and another one very soon."

Stunned into silence at Valentino's confession, Dean's hands came together and began the wringing process.

He had to stop this demented man, and now.

Could he get his gun before Valentino shot him? Probably not, but he was going to try.

He had no choice. There was far more revealed in his words than a serial killer confession. This man knew the BAU, and he was exceedingly clever. This complete setup proved it. He had known what was coming, how law enforcement worked, and planned accordingly.

Now or never, Deano.

Just as he was ready to make his move, they rolled to a stop.

"We've arrived, Agent."

Dean glanced through the windshield and saw the headlights uncover the small, blue car parked on the side of the road. No doubt, Valentino's getaway car.

The gun was suddenly against his temple.

"First, law enforcement disrespects me and my noble purpose by calling me insane. I tried to accept that for what it is, ignorance, but I couldn't let it go entirely. Yes, I was able to finally make a peace with that. She and her boyfriend are now going to be very famous because of my ability to forgive and love.

"But, now, after trying to set the record straight with your BAU, and then being shot for it, I realize that my battle will only become more difficult if I don't do what is necessary."

There was no ignoring the edge of contempt that had slipped into Valentino's voice. Under his guise of love and creativity, he was beginning to show his true self. Dean felt the dread engulf him.

"What does that mean?"

"It means what it means," Valentino said, pulling the gun away from Dean's head.

Dean dove for the weapon. Almost simultaneously, he heard the quick report from the Berretta as it rocked the inside of the SUV. Then nothing at all.

CHAPTER-29

Belle sat down in the leather chair, trying to control her nerves, and succeeding for the most part. It had been a quick trip form Bradshaw International Airport, but the memories, good and bad, had overwhelmed her.

There was still nothing like the ambiance and beauty of a palm-tree-filled Caribbean island. The warmth, the green, the sound of the waves rolling to shore and the contrasting terrains of mountains and valleys weaving their own magic were enchanting. But her favorite part of being here had always been the scent of ocean and flora as they converged. She swore she still smelled it during the winter in her apartment from time to time.

Yet, here, underneath that beauty lay a demon that had to be exorcised for both her and Cammy's sake. She knew that. She and Josh had talked about it, but talking and doing were worlds apart, or at least had been until this moment.

She rested her hands on her stomach, hoping to calm the tiny dragons causing havoc there. She could, and would, do this, even if it meant she would spend the rest of her life in a loony bin or staring at the bottom of a bottle of booze.

Josh seemed to sense her thoughts and reached over to whisper in her ear.

"We've got this together, remember?"

She nodded and then smiled at the two men sitting across from them.

The assistant commissioner of police for the SNK, Angus Dirks, a lean, forty-something man with dark hair and even darker skin, owning a demeanor that reminded her more of a politician than a cop, sat on the other side of the desk. He was accompanied by an older, pudgy gentleman who could only be retired Inspector Gaylord Jamison.

"We want to thank you for meeting with us so late, but I assure you, it's of utmost importance," said Josh.

The man could be as charming as a movie star.

"It is no problem," said Dirks.

"Kind of you to say. As I said on the phone, Special Agent Simmons and I are here to pick your brains regarding a cold case murder on your island that happened over twenty years ago.

Dirks and the inspector looked at each other. Finally, Dirks gave Jamison a brief nod.

Jamison leaned over the great wooden desk toward Belle. His dark eyes still sparkled after twenty years, but the light in them couldn't completely mask his sadness.

"How are you doin', Belle? I didn't tink I would see you agin."

"As well as can be expected, thank you. I didn't think I'd be back."

"I am glad to hear dat. Da last time we spoke was not under such good circumstances, but I taut you would be fine. You were tough even den."

"Thank you again."

She opened her mouth to say that she hadn't wanted to be tough, just a girl on vacation enjoying her new friends. Seeing one of them murdered hadn't been on her vacation itinerary. She stopped herself from commenting on this and instead stayed her course.

"I do my best."

"'Tis all any of us can do."

Josh leaned forward, elbows on knees. "I don't mean to interrupt the reunion, but will you help us? We have a runaway killer in Miami, and we want to stop him, now."

Again, Jamison and Dirks exchanged telltale glances.

Dirks leaned back in his chair, his hands clasped behind his head.

"Agent Corner. We have sent all we have to the FBI so that poor Cammy's murderer might someday be caught. While that horrible day has in some ways scarred our island, we have done our best, including her family, to move forward. Inspector Jamison and his staff did all they could to find this attacker. Why do you think we can help you further?"

There was some snap in Dirks's voice.

Interesting.

"Because, Assistant Commissioner, as you well know, not everything that transpires in a case like this is included in a report or a form, or even in crime scene photos. People have interacted with people, and that is what we're here to discuss, hopefully to unearth something that will help us," said Josh, staying cool and collected.

Belle never took her eyes from the men. She prayed she would see something in either of them to indicate that Josh was on to something.

She didn't have to wait long.

Dirks's countenance shifted and his body took on an air of defense.

"Do you think we purposely omitted information that would have helped in this investigation, Special Agent?"

Standing, Josh moved to the desk, sitting on the corner of it.

"I think that a crime like this, with a prime witness describing a suspect that surely had to fit a limited number of people on the island at that time, shouldn't have gone unsolved. In fact, it should have been wrapped up in a few hours, by my estimation," said Josh.

"So you believe we know who her killer was, do you not?" asked Dirks, his voice rising.

"I'll answer that," said Belle.

She hadn't intended to release twenty years of fear, anger, and frustration in this meeting. It wasn't even on her radar, the conscious one at least, but all of those memories, sleepless nights, and crying spells molded into one point of energy. Belle Simmons exploded.

"Yes, you bastards, yes. You had to know," she yelled. "How many teenage white boys were on this damn island then? Five? Ten?"

"Who do you think—" Dirks began.

Diving over the desk, Belle grabbed Dirks by his island shirt and pulled his face to hers, his eyes the size of hubcaps.

"I'm the girl who will never forget what she saw in that cave, you prick. Now tell me who killed her."

A moment later, she felt Josh's strong hands grip her sides and lift her in the air, but she refused to let go of Dirks's shirt.

"Answer me. Who killed her?"

"Belle, let go of him," said Josh.

"No! He knows. Damn him, he knows."

She wiggled free from her boss and tightened her grip. She thought she might bite his face if he didn't answer her.

Another hand then touched her face, and she turned quickly to see Jamison looking at her with the love of a father and the shame of a sinner.

Time stood frozen in place until Jamison finally spoke.

"His name is Eric Tovant, Belle. Eric Tovant killed our Cammy."

CHAPTER-30

The darkened SUV sat ominously beside the two-lane, almost taunting them.

The GPS on Sophie's phone read that both Dean and his phone were in the same place, and the FBI's vehicle seemed to be it.

"Here?" asked Sophie, but she already knew the answer.

"Yes."

She pulled the cruiser off the road, flipped on the flashing lights, then pulled up to within twenty feet of the SUV.

"Watch my ass," she said, and then was out the door before Manny could stop her.

They'd talked about being careful if this situation came up, and he hoped she would keep that conversation in the forefront of her mind.

He swung his door open, Glock in hand, and hurried to the driver's side of the vehicle. Sophie was almost to the passenger's side, so he stepped it up.

They should be more cautious than this. Who knew what Valentino might have done? But Manny dismissed it. Bombs and traps weren't this man's style. Besides, Manny would have to shoot Sophie to slow her down at this point.

When they both reached the backseats, Sophie called out, "Anything?"

"Nothing yet."

"Okay . . . oh no, no."

His partner's voice went from strong to barely audible.

"What?" he yelled, not able to mask the fear in his voice as he sprinted around the front of the truck.

The door was open, and Manny panicked even more because he didn't see Sophie at first. Then he saw movement and realized she had crawled inside.

Two more steps, and he was around the door.

He stopped moving, dropping the gun to his side, unable to comprehend what he was seeing at first. Reality was a sobering entity without any prejudice.

The tears began falling in hot rivulets as Manny followed the streaks of fresh blood on the armrest of the door to more blood on the floor mat and then up to the seat where Dean Mikus lay in Sophie's arms, more crimson liquid flowered against his paisley shirt.

His eyes were closed as if he were in the midst of a contented sleep.

Sophie was speaking softly to him, her mouth so very close to his ear, her tone filled with love and comfort while she cradled him jealously in her small lap, stroking his hair.

"He shot my Dean, Manny," she said softly without looking up.

More tears flowed as he steadied himself against the open door.

How does anyone describe heartache like that? He understood it, what Sophie was feeling. Louise had died in his arms, but to describe it would require far more understanding than he'd achieved in this life, maybe not in any life.

Manny knew what to do in most any circumstance, to think rationally and execute the plan. It was part of his gift. But here, now, he was at a loss. He stared helplessly at his best friend and her husband.

They weren't cops or special agents now, but two people who had fallen in love. Manny had been there when they exchanged vows, when they swore to take care of each other until the very end.

Never did he believe the end would come so soon for either of them.

Reaching out to try to comfort Sophie, he pulled his hand back in utter surprise.

Dean had opened his eyes.

CHAPTER-31

Removing his shirt, he dropped it in the bathroom sink. He leaned toward the mirror to get a better look at where the bullet had grazed his shoulder.

The wound had bled some and was a little deeper than he'd hoped, but nothing he couldn't patch up. He'd live, and that was all that mattered.

Valentino reached for the first-aid case and went to work. Fifteen minutes later, he stepped back and grinned. Not bad, not bad at all. It barely hurt. Once again, he'd found a hidden talent.

He brushed the hair from his eyes and stared at his reflection. Talent was something he had, and he wanted the world to know. He hadn't felt this way initially, but he'd changed over the last twelve hours. His ideals had suffered a blow when the black bitch called him crazy, and that triggered something in him.

His love to serve and immortalize others was still strong. No matter what the cops or FBI did, that wouldn't change. But now, his awakening had taken another step, and he wanted people to know the artist as well as the art.

Mission accomplished.

His picture would be all over the state, the country, and maybe even the world in a matter of hours. They would know his name. Hell, even his Miami address.

But not everything is as it seems.

Savvy Internet users would search for him, learn about what he'd done. He would enlighten them even further with links to his art. And not just the visions from his first two true creations, but the third one the BAU had not discovered as of yet.

"I'll need to fix that if they don't find it soon," he said out loud.

But first, he had something else to finish before he could embrace the next step in his evolution.

After one last look in the mirror, he reached for the blue carrying case he had left in the hotel room a few hours before going to the warehouse.

As he unzipped the side pocket, it hit him.

The intense pain in his head drove him to his knees and onto the cool tile of the bathroom floor while his world grew hazy causing his world to spin out of control. The instantaneous and overwhelming nausea threatened to encourage his stomach to spew its contents.

He tried to control the pain, hoping the queasiness would follow suit, like all of those times before. He could do it if—

The unwanted movie began showing inside his head, another hideous rerun from his childhood spawned from that hellish place. It squelched his hopes of any control he might exercise and finished off what was left of his resolve.

Crouching near the fringe of the small clearing, he was hidden from view of the three grown-ups by the wild, thick undergrowth. He wanted to approach them and tell them he had been chasing butterflies and got separated from his father, but he was afraid of them. After all, they were black and his father had told him black people were trouble. He stayed put.

He could see and hear them but, at age eight, he wasn't entirely sure what they were discussing.

The pretty woman, hair rustling in the island's breeze, held the hand of the younger man. The older, larger man in the white hat gestured to one then the other. The older man's actions reminded him of when his mother and father were speaking to him about something he'd done wrong.

With an abruptness that caused him to jump, the older man began yelling at the girl, and then he hit her, sending her flying to the ground.

"No," yelled the younger man and hit the older man with his fist.

The boy flinched and began to cry. He'd never seen such violence before. It wasn't like getting into a fight at recess. Not at all like that.

The movie played on.

"Stop. He is my father," said the young woman, rising to her feet.

The young man stepped back, his hands in the air in an apologetic pose while the older man struggled to his feet.

After he wiped blood from the corner of his mouth, he told his daughter to come to him. She hesitated and then she did.

The accompanying hug seemed genuine.

"I love you my daughter. I only want what is best for you."

"I know, Papa. I know. But I love him."

He nodded at his girl, then looked at the younger man with something that the boy would learn later to be true hatred.

The older man took the older revolver from his pocket and began shooting.

After each horrific roar from the gun, he stepped closer and shot again, even after the young man was on the ground, unmoving.

In those bushes, something came alive in him, and he stopped crying.

He knew he should run away and find his father. To let him know that he was safe and to tell him what he'd seen. He could have gotten away, no one would have seen him, but the strange, unexplainable curiosity welling in him had been awakened. He wanted to see what was coming next.

The daughter stood in shocked silence, her look as unforgettable as the setting of the day.

Without hesitating, her father turned back to his daughter.

"I did what I had to do because I love you and don't want to see you suffer. This man was poison," he said.

Her lip began to quiver, tears already staining her pink blouse.

"You love me? That's how you show your love for me? I spit on you. You killed him, the man I love and the father of your grandchild."

"What? You are pregnant?"

He didn't wait for her to answer. The rage on his face wouldn't allow it.

Reaching her, he pulled her to his chest and then shot her in the head. He pulled the trigger again, and then again, before he placed her gently on the sandy ground.

Still hidden, the boy watched intently, his heart beating like a race horse, his excitement unmeasurable, and his anticipation off the charts.

The older man then dropped to his knees, his face serene, as he took his daughter's bloodied hand.

"I love you. I love you. I had to make you see this man was only heartache and hell for you. Now you will rest in peace."

After kissing her, the man looked up and somehow saw him through the brush.

Their eyes locked, and then he offered the boy a tiny grin before raising the gun to his head and pulling the trigger.

Unable to resist the compulsion that drove him, even if he wanted to, he left his hiding place and approached the bodies of the man and his daughter.

Her face was mostly intact, as was her father's, as they lay in pooling blood, touching each other's hand.

So this was love?

His mother and father always told him that they loved them, but he never really understood until now, this very moment, what love was truly about. He wanted to have love like that. The thrill of it all was not totally within his grasp, but it would be. He was sure of that.

He saw himself stepping away from the clearing, a new outlook on life and love buried deep within his psyche.

He quickly found another butterfly to follow, and the chase brought him to his frantic father.

Good old dad hugged him fiercely, and even though he was angry with his son, he told him he loved him.

For the first time in the boy's life, he had a true sense of what love was. Love meant doing whatever you had to do to make it better for the ones you loved. Even at that tender age, he had begun the journey of expressing that truth in his own special way.

There was no message telling him that the movie had ended, no scrolling cast list.

Immediately, his head began to clear and his stomach settled enough that he was able to rise from the floor. His recovery time from these events had improved over the years, but he wondered about the effects of the intense migraines. Then again, did it matter? He thought not for what he had in mind.

Another look in the mirror revealed a paler reflection of the man who'd been there previously, but the memory, if not the pain and nausea, had helped him to refocus on his self-expectations.

He reached for the case again, removing the scissors, the razor, and the bottle of dye.

CHAPTER-32

For the third time on this trip, Belle began to speak to Josh, but he held up his hand and then engaged in two brief calls.

Zealous to discuss the meeting hardly described what was going on with her.

She and Josh hadn't spoken more than ten words after they left the Saint Kitts's police building, mostly because Josh was concerned with what their driver might overhear as they were taken back to the airport. Belle understood that. But they'd been in the air for ten minutes, and he hadn't given her the time of day.

There was another reason they weren't speaking—in Belle's eyes, at least. Her boss was distracted by something else.

His hushed tones, the quick, insincere smiles after he hung up and apologized for not hearing her, and last but not least, the look of concern on his face that he was not able to hide.

She listened, drinking her coffee, and waited for him to finish his call.

"You just stick with the plan . . ."

She heard that much before he disconnected the call and then swiveled in his chair to face her. This time there was no attempt to mask anything.

Josh Corner had always been enjoyable and professional with a touch of charm that added to his already-obvious physical appeal, but at that moment, he was dealing with some frustration.

She wanted to ask him questions about the meeting, about why he didn't press the island police more after the story, and why he didn't mention the idea of pressing charges against the officials on the island for allowing Tovant to protect his only son.

He hadn't even threatened to fire her for grabbing Dirks by the shirt.

After forcing her to face her worst fear, *almost* forcing her anyway, he owed her some of his time.

She felt the heat crawl up her neck to her cheeks. She wanted some damned answers, now.

Josh tilted his head, no smile to be found, his voice almost far away.

"I'm sorry, Belle. I know we should talk about a few things and how they were handled, and we will, but we have some different issues right now."

"Like what, Josh? It better be good. You and Manny sent me to the hellhole that almost drove me crazy years ago, and now you're telling me we have some 'different issues' to take care of? That's not fair."

"I know. Like I said, we can talk later. I just found out that a side assignment I have taken initiative to handle isn't where it should be. But more important than that, for now, is the fact that Dean's been shot and is fighting for his life."

Belle felt her jaw drop, then instantaneous shame at her own selfishness for demanding her own way without getting all of the details from Josh.

"Oh God in heaven. What happened?"

"Manny only said that Valentino set them up somehow at the warehouse, stole the SUV with Dean in it. Sophie and Manny tracked the SUV and finally found it—with Dean at death's door in the passenger's seat. He's in surgery to repair perforated intestines. It could take hours."

"So he's going to be all right?"

Josh stared without focus at the floor of the jet, the sound of rushing air as ominous as wind in a cemetery.

"There's only about a twenty-percent chance he'll make it."

Having her stomach twist in this business wasn't all that unusual, but the knot in her belly now made her nauseated.

"Twenty percent?"

"There's more. Even if they can reach the bullet and he survives, the doctors don't believe he'll walk again."

CHAPTER-33

The ride to Miami's largest hospital had been like a roller coaster that traveled from somewhere high into heaven straight into the deepest, darkest depths of hell for Sophie.

Dean was still alive, and the EMS got to the SUV in no time flat.

Heaven.

Her odd, but incredible, loving husband had even spoken to her. He said he loved her and not to worry. He even joked that he'd bled more than this the last time he shaved his beard.

Heaven, again.

Halfway to the hospital, Dean's eyes had rolled up into his head, only showing the whites, and his blood pressure and heart rate had fallen off a cliff. The EMS crew was very skilled and brought him out of it, but they had no repair for the years that episode had taken from her life.

Hell.

When they finally rolled into the emergency circle in front of the entrance, her spirits spiked high again—higher than they should have. She had been holding his hand, kissing it incessantly, when Dean's heart stopped completely.

Hell again.

After two horrible minutes and three AED shock treatments, his heart began beating.

Heaven.

She looked down into the small cup of shitty hospital coffee, her mind going in every direction and nowhere at all.

What would she do if he didn't come through the surgery? How could she breathe? How would she be able to put one foot in front of the other?

Thoughts of Manny dealing with Louise's death came to her.

She'd cried with him, held him, and even joked with him, making every attempt to console in her own way. At the time, she thought she understood what he was going through.

Not even close. She understood jack shit.

"Any updates?" asked Manny.

Turning to her right, she saw her friend walking into the waiting room from the hallway where he'd been meeting with Miami law enforcement.

"No. Nothing yet. I keep asking, but they just say the same thing. If I go up to that desk one more time, they'll probably give me a shot to put me under and then cuff me to one of those beds in the psych ward."

"What? You don't want them to do that? I mean, there was a time when that handcuff thing appealed to you, right?"

She shook her head slowly, unable to stop the tiny smile.

"True. But I can wait this time."

Then Sophie melted into Manny's strong arms and let him hold her.

All her life, she had been tough, hard, and self-reliant, bottling up her frustrations and anger for her own good . . . and never showing anyone the essence of who she really was.

But not with Manny—not that it would have done a lot of good trying to hide her thoughts from him anyway, his gift made that impossible.

Beyond seeing her for who she was, he accepted her, cared for her, and loved her completely, even right from the start of their partnership.

No bullshit, no pretense, just utter acceptance for who she was and where she was in her life. No one, not even her parents and siblings, made her feel like that.

If the God he talked about from time to time held those traits, and Manny said He did, then she was grateful He'd given them to Manny, especially now.

There was never a romantic side to their relationship, although she'd held a secret infatuation for a brief time.

He was just Manny, the Big Brother that everyone should have.

"Dean's got this you know? He's a hell of a fighter and loves his life with you," whispered Manny.

Fresh tears spilled from her eyes as she squeezed tighter.

"You'd better be right, or I'm going to kick both your asses."

"Duly noted. And in case you hadn't noticed, I'm right a lot."

"Yes, you are."

A few minutes later, she released her grip and touched his hard chest.

"Sorry about the tear stains. I'll get you another shirt."

"I'll live. But I do have a favor to ask," said Manny.

"As long as it has to do with killing Valentino's ugly ass, fire away."

"Well, it does have to do with him. Are you able to talk about a few things regarding this case?"

"Yeah. I think so. I can't box up my emotions like you, but I can be a cop, I think."

Manny nodded. "Good. Although, I'm not sure how good of a job I'm doing boxing up my emotions either."

There was no mistaking the edge in Manny's voice as he spoke. She'd seen him pissed, especially the night he'd taken Argyle out, but still . . .

He read her mind, again.

"Yes, I'm fighting this damn angry attitude that I can't quite get a grip on. I think I've been that way since before we left Lansing, but I'm good."

"If you say so."

"I do. Ready?"

"As ready as I'll ever be."

"If you say so."

"Don't mock me."

"I wasn't, in the true sense of mocking."

"Yeah? Okay then, let's get this going."

There was another of those magical smiles. That made her forget her problems for a second or two. He got another A+ for trying.

"Josh called to give us the name of the suspect that the Saint Kitts police believe killed Belle's friend."

"What? They knew?"

"Apparently. Josh said it was complicated and had to do with money and politics and the man who owned the sugar transportation company that employed a ton of Saint Kitts's workers. He said they're still working though some more details, but that's not our concern for now. We have to find Eric Tovant."

Sophie ran the name through her mind a dozen times in a few seconds, allowing him to sink in.

Eric Tovant had killed at least six Miami innocents and one poor little island girl. He'd shot her husband, who was struggling desperately not to be the next Tovant victim.

Her heart was ravaged with another wave of fear, doubt, and lastly, rage, at the idea that Dean, who wouldn't harm another if his life depended on it, might not see another sunrise.

She clenched and unclenched her hands repeatedly, trying to find hope in the middle of that possibility.

Manny always talked about doing things the right way and letting the system work. Everyone had a right to justice. No matter what they'd done. If not, then the system wasn't good or fair for anyone.

Right now, she couldn't care less for anyone else's definition of that overused and under practiced ideal.

This man needed to die.

She glanced up at Manny, searching those blues for a little direction, if not redemption for her runaway anger and ideas of revenge.

There wasn't any.

His eyes were almost a reflection of her very thoughts. "Almost" being the operative word. Men like Manny would always have a small measure of compassion and empathy for a perp, no matter what the killer had done—because they couldn't help it.

But she wasn't cut that way.

"What do you want me to do? As much as I'd like to cut this man's balls off and feed them to him as I cut out his heart, I can't leave Dean," she said.

"I appreciate the sentiments, and I would never ask you to leave Dean. I'm not sure I can leave you both, but we have to get to this man while the getting might be good."

She nodded.

"So far we've not been able to truly ID Valentino as Eric Tovant."

"You're not convinced?"

"I've found that being convinced of something and discovering the truth can be two different things entirely."

"Meaning what?"

"Meaning I need you to hold down the fort until Belle and Josh get back from Saint Kitts. I want you to look at the data that comes in on Eric Tovant from the FBI's databases and whatever else we have from Miami-Dade's research division plus the files from the island's police department. There are two forensic units out to the warehouse where you shot Valentino collecting whatever they can, including blood samples to compare DNA against CODIS to see if there's a match and make sense of the rest of it."

"Are you being cautious or is your brain doing one of those 'pull applesauce out of a pile of shit' things again?" she asked.

"If you mean do I want to make sure black is black here, then yes. Something seems a little off with the manner in which Valentino made himself so visible when it wasn't in his make-up, at least as far as I was concerned. And he no doubt talked about 'why' with Dean before he was shot. Which also leads me to think he didn't intend to shoot Dean."

"Why do you say that? I mean about shooting Dean. I think I get it about probably talking about getting his rocks off killing people, hell, they all do that, but explain yourself."

He draped a strong arm around Sophie's shoulders.

"You'd already have that figured out if you didn't have more important things to be concerned with. Two things here. Why kill Dean if he told him about himself? Wouldn't he have wanted Dean to help spread the word?

"The other thing is the angle of the shot to Dean's middle indicates the barrel of the gun was lower so the shot went upward. If Valentino was just going to kill Dean, he would have probably shot from his shoulder height and probably not aimed for the stomach either. I almost think Dean made a play for the gun."

Sophie felt another flush of tears well up thinking about how brave that action had been for her husband.

"I know you're right. I can just see him doing it, that dumbass. I told him to never try to be a hero like that because he sucks at it."

"He's a cop, you know? He did what he thought was the right thing to do."

She sighed. "I know. I know."

She felt his gentle kiss on her head.

"He's going to make it, Sophie. He's a good man and tougher than most," Manny said softly.

"Yeah, that's what scares me. It seems like God takes all of the good ones and leaves the rest of us to figure out why."

"Not this time. We need him."

Funny how Manny said "we." But then again, that's how he looked at things. They were a team, a family, always.

"Okay, I have to keep my mind off that emergency surgery room so I'll do it. Just no guarantees, but I'll do my best."

"Good. The local officers brought us a laptop programmed for just this kind of thing so when I leave, they'll bring it in."

She had known he was going to leave, but hearing it was tougher than she'd imagined. Alone with the prospects of terrible news on the horizon wasn't her idea of a good time, but she understood her partner, didn't she? Guardians of the Universe saw a bigger picture.

"I'll only be a phone call away," he said, once again in tune with her emotions. "We have to stop this killer before any more murders."

"Okay. I get that. What are you going to be doing?"

"I'm leaving with Marie and Duane to search Eric Tovant's house. He owns one on the northeast side of Miami. It had belonged to his parents, both deceased by the way."

"You don't think this psycho left you any clues about what's next for his screwed-up love and kill agenda, do you?"

Manny looked out the window into the night sky, then back to her, a tense smile clouding his handsome face.

"I think we just might find more than we bargained for."

CHAPTER-34

The pin-sized light coming from the end of the dark passageway seemed miles away. It was barely distinguishable.

He immediately thought about the stories of people who claimed they had near-death experiences. In almost every version of their encounters, they had been plunged into immediate darkness until a bright light drew them through a distant tunnel. The light eventually grew to the point where it completely bathed them in a great white light. Then, they would be introduced to a close relative, or maybe Jesus Himself.

Alex wondered what Manny would think if he knew that Alex had been curious enough about his God to actually do research on the end-of-life experience.

He'd probably smile and say something like, "It's about time."

So was this the end? Was he dead? He couldn't remember much of what had happened after the surgery to attach the new hand. Nothing much at all.

Barb? Did he see her? Did they talk? Maybe. That felt right, though his grasp on reality was questionable at best right now.

The light began to grow brighter, expanding to almost encompass him, but it was blurry and out of kilter.

After realizing that he probably was still alive, he reached unsteadily with his right hand and made a valiant effort to wipe the fog from his eyes. He missed and slapped himself on the nose.

That seemed to do the trick, however. His vision began to focus and then cleared faster than a New York minute as his immediate surroundings came into perfect view.

The white-walled room was much smaller than his original hospital abode although it seemed to be clean and fully capable of handling a patient's needs, he hoped. He'd just had a major surgery; it wouldn't be good for him if he were wrong.

There was one double-paned window to his right, a bathroom directly in front of him some ten feet away. To the left of that was a door he assumed led out of the room.

There was a black padded chair near the foot of the bed on the left, where several wires and tubes were running into the extreme porcupine metal cast on his arm, and one chair on his right side.

In the chair on the right was a purse. He recognized it as the designer bag he'd bought Barb for Christmas last year.

Shaking the last of the cobwebs from his mind, he eventually got around to wondering why he was here and not in his original room. Was this a special recovery room? If so, why wasn't he told about it? But that was the government for you, right? They never told anyone squat.

Barb.

Where in hell was she?

She wouldn't leave him alone in a situation like this, ever.

He frowned. They'd had a discussion and almost an argument, hadn't they? It was about the last time he'd come to Walter Reed. Was she that pissed at him? He'd missed something in their conversation, he was sure of that, but she wouldn't leave him alone, right?

His eyes blurred over again. He blinked, held them shut for a few seconds, then opened them again.

The door swung open, and two people entered just as his vision cleared for a second time.

It didn't matter, nor did he care, that he didn't recognize the large, pale, white man with the shaved head wearing a black suit and tie to match. He only cared about the woman who made his heart leap. Seeing his wife sent waves of relief coursing over his body; there was no one on earth he wanted to see more.

She moved to the chair, set her purse on the floor, and took his hand.

"How you doing, tiger?"

"I'm coming around. Where am I? This isn't my room at the hospital."

Barb glanced at the big man.

"No it's not. I, we, couldn't leave you there."

Alex opened his mouth to ask why, then he remembered everything, especially Barb poking him with a hypodermic needle and the lights going out. What the hell was that about?

"Raise my bed up so I can look you in the face while you tell me why you shot me up with something and why we're someplace other than where I'm supposed to be."

Barb reached for the remote and adjusted the bed so that he was sitting at almost a right angle, then she sat back down.

The man cleared his throat but said nothing.

Alex shot him a look, then turned back to his wife.

"Well?" he asked. "Do I have to play fifty questions or some other pointless game?"

"There is more going on here involving you and your surgery, Alex."

"I gather that. Keep talking."

She reached for his hand, and he pulled it away.

"Talk."

She nodded.

"You were right when we talked before your surgery. I have never lied to you before, that minute, ever, and it almost killed me when they wheeled you into the operating room with that black mark on my report card, but I had to."

"You had to? Why?"

"I was protecting you. You couldn't know what was in store for you after the surgery."

Alex felt like his head was going to explode.

This cryptic conversation was driving him toward goofy land.

"You really need to get to the point. I'm going a bit crazy here. You make this sound like some top-secret, double-probation mission or something."

There was another glance at the large man standing by the door. He still hadn't moved and seemed to have no desire to speak to Alex.

"Something like that. Let me explain. Last year, when you two were on your way to Las Vegas, Josh did do what you saw and gave me an address and something to do."

"So I was right. And I remember that you were smiling like you were doing a toothpaste commercial."

"I was, but that was a show for you. Where I had to go and what I had to do were far away from anything fun. That kind of thing never is."

Watching her body language and the calm demeanor of her voice, Alex felt as if he had slipped into another world. Although this was his loving wife of twelve years sitting in that chair, she wasn't just that anymore. There was more to her than even he had realized.

"What does that mean, Barb?"

"It means there are some people out there who want to do more harm than good, especially to you after your surgery, and Josh and I couldn't let that happen."

"Me? Why? Wait, don't answer that. You've been a stay-at-home wife since we've been married. Why would Josh tell you something that he didn't tell me? I don't get this connection."

Barb exhaled. "I don't expect you to understand, honey, but it's a little more complicated than that."

There was a knock on the door; the man in the black suit moved to the side as the door swung open.

An even larger black man entered the door, hair in dreadlocks, sporting an island shirt that exposed a sample of his massive chest and arms.

Alex felt his jaw drop to his chest. He recognized the man from their trip to Puerto Rico.

What was he doing out of prison? He shouldn't be here. He should still be rotting away for the shit he pulled on Manny and the rest of them regarding Argyle's little experiment on mind control.

"What she's tryin' to tell you mon is that she works for the government, and I don't mean in da IRS office," said Braxton Smythe.

CHAPTER-35

The smallish bungalow stood dark, inside and out. The bluish sedan was the only object near the house to indicate someone actually lived there.

The street lights, and the glow of the waxing full moon, offered them a measure of light. It was enough for what they needed to do.

They had discussed how to approach the home so there was no need for last-minute adjustments. Watching each other's asses was always a given. They were ready.

Manny winked at Marie. She winked back and smiled, something he hadn't seen her do often. She wore it well. He and three blues went to work and began the regimen of circling to the back of the house while Marie, Duane, and two other officers staked out the front.

Approaching the car, Manny put his hand on the hood. It wasn't hot by any means, like it had just been running, just warm to the touch. He wouldn't have expected less in the Miami climate. He motioned for the others to continue.

After they had worked their way around both sides of the house, finding no one inside of the small blue Ford parked in the driveway, he motioned for the three to form a semicircle some fifteen feet from the screened backdoor that led to the small cement lanai.

There were potted bougainvillea trees guarding each side of the door on the inside of the screened area. They were accompanied by two padded wicker chairs that were placed neatly on each side of the small glass table, but that was all Manny could see.

It appeared that Valentino lived a simple life away from the hell and destruction he'd caused.

"I don't see anything on this end," said Marie, her voice cascading through the earpieces they had all been equipped with before they arrived.

Reaching for the small mic fastened to the lapel of his Kevlar vest, he pulled it closer.

"We don't see any movement from the back. There wasn't anything or anyone suspicious or out of the ordinary as we made our way back along the sides of the house either."

"Should we go then?"

The butterflies of excitement and paradoxical anxiety fluttered with purpose inside Manny's gut. Maybe they'd get lucky. Maybe this dickhead was fast asleep in his bed, believing he had escaped the obvious by being obvious.

One could dream.

Yet, the killer had to know law enforcement would come to this house—to forensically process Eric Tovant's domicile and try to piece together a reason for his killing. Those would be normal procedures he would expect.

Was Valentino counting on the cops showing up? If so, why?

"I think it's your call, Marie. I don't like how this feels though."

"Yeah, I hear you. Then again, we say that every time we do this, right?"

"I know, but this man is not a fool and he had to know we would come a knocking."

"Yes. But like we talked about, setting a trap or placing a bomb or some shit doesn't appear to be his style."

Manny thought about what she said, and she was right.

Even though he'd almost trapped them at the warehouse, Valentino had wanted to explain his nobility and his method, not kill them. Was that the extent of his purpose? Probably, but who could tell for sure if Dean's kidnap was just an unfortunate circumstance or something else?

He decided that the owner of this house wasn't that clever.

"Okay. Just watch your butts. I still don't like this."

"All right. Ready? On three. One-two-three."

Pulling on the back door, Manny swung it open. The three blues rushed in front of him, leading to what looked like the kitchen.

"Clear," yelled the first blue.

The second officer found the light switch on the wall just as Manny heard the front door burst open.

The kitchen light broke the semi-darkness, revealing a tiny, clean kitchen. He took one more step when shouting escalated from the front of the house.

At first, he didn't understand what was happening, then he did.

"Get out, now, dammit. I said—" yelled Marie.

The rapid fire of what Manny recognized as an AK-47 exploded from somewhere in the front of the house, blotting out Marie Swifton's next words.

CHAPTER-36

"Did you both have a great time?" asked Chloe.

She'd been sitting at the table going over arrest reports from the Lansing Police Department after she'd put Ian down for the count when Haley Rose and Jen came through the door carrying more than the usual bags filled with mall merchandise.

"Oh yeah," said Jen. "I'm going to get chewed out for going over my allowance on Dad's credit card, but the summer outfits were so cute. I couldn't help myself."

"Aye, I can vouch for that. The lass *does* look fine in all of those outfits, don't you know," said Haley Rose, grinning.

The trouble these two had endured over the last couple of months seemed to have vanished for the moment, and Chloe's heart was lifted to see it.

She'd bet her next check that the last thing Manny would be worried about was a little overspending from his daughter.

He had other things on his mind, including the text after they'd talked this afternoon with a picture of what she wasn't wearing. Then again, when he was deep in a case, nothing seemed to distract him much for very long.

Shoving aside the files, she motioned for Jen to put her bags on the table.

"Let's take a look. But I want to see the prom dress first."

Jen looked at Haley Rose, who nodded at her.

"Well. I didn't buy one," Jen said.

"You didn't? Why not? I thought that was the big ticket item."

"Well. I talked it over with Granny and decided that I wanted you to go with me and pick it out, if you're good with that, okay?"

The sudden rush of emotion took Chloe by surprise.

She'd loved Jen since the first time they'd sat down to talk about Chloe being her stepmom and Manny's second wife.

They'd talked honestly, directly, and with caring respect concerning Louise's place in Jen's heart and Chloe's place in her new life. Chloe would be there for her whenever she needed her, but understood she could never replace Louise and would never try to force the issue.

At times, she felt as if they'd grown closer, especially since Ian had been born, and it was wonderful to journey there, but often she didn't truly know where she stood with Jen.

Now she felt she knew.

Jen's eyes were shining, and Chloe knew her own eyes were a match. She stood and hugged Manny's daughter.

"I would be honored to help you with that," she whispered.

"Cool. That's really cool."

Then Jen gave her an extra tight squeeze before stepping back.

"We can go tomorrow morning, if you like. Granny said she'll watch the munchkin."

"That's a date."

"Okay then. I'm going to take my haul into my room, and I'll try on the stuff so you can see."

"Ahh. I told you lass, you look fine in all of it, but it won't hurt to have another eye, now will it. Get along now."

Gathering her packages and bags, Jen went to her room to change. Sampson, who had been quiet until he saw her leaving for her room, padded behind her.

"She's quite a young'un," said Haley Rose.

Immediately, Chloe turned to face her mother. Haley Rose's tone had made Chloe's heart jump.

Her mum was distraught suddenly.

"Mum? Are ya all right?"

Haley Rose turned to her, tears in her eyes, but her jaw set at the same time. Chloe had seen that look more than once while growing up in Galway. Her mum's stubborn, determined mindset had resurfaced. She felt herself cringe inside.

"No. I'm not all right. I'm tired of the way I feel. I'm tired of not getting m'self balanced out."

"What does that mean?"

"It means I have some unfinished business, and after Jen's prom next week, I'll be heading back to Ireland."

Chloe was shocked. "What? Why are you doing that, Mum? I thought you loved it here."

"I do. It'll be hard on me, don't ya know. I love both of these babies. But I ain't doing what I've been trying to do anymore."

Chloe stepped closer, but her mum backed away a step.

"Mum. Whatever that is, we can help."

Haley Rose's eyes narrowed. "Can ya now? You can take what's left of my sanity and patch that up along with the pieces of my broken heart? Ya can work those kind of miracles?"

"No. I can't, but there are ways to make it better. I know what you've gone through. I'll do whatever it takes to see you feel better."

"Whatever? Whatever darling?" Haley Rose asked softly.

Chloe frowned. For the first time in years, she felt unsettled speaking with her mum.

"Yes. I said that."

Exhaling, Haley Rose smiled a humorless smile.

"Yes, ya did. But I don't need your help anymore. I'll do this my way. Stay out of it, darlin'. Do ya hear me?"

Before Chloe could answer, Jen's door opened and she paraded down the hallway in one of her new outfits.

Her mother turned away and followed Jen as she entered the kitchen.

"My, don't ya look like an angel," said Haley Rose.

Her mum shifted from witch to loving grandmother so fast Chloe almost wondered if she'd heard correctly.

That wasn't all she was wondering. She would talk to Manny tonight or tomorrow when he checked in, but if she didn't know better, she thought Haley Rose might be standing on the precipice of a nervous breakdown.

Watching her with Jen, she shook it off. Her mum was tired and still stinging from some of life's haymakers. She'd be better tomorrow, right?

CHAPTER-37

The second roar from the AK-47 sent Manny scurrying to his knees.

"Down. Get down!" he yelled.

The stream of bullets that ripped through the thin walls sprayed drywall and wood on top of Manny and two of the other officers who had hit the deck with him.

The third cop wasn't so fortunate. He'd stared at Manny with puzzlement and was too slow in reacting to his warning.

A moment later, that man was a mess, blood pouring on the hardwood floor, his body virtually ripped in half by the burst from the assault rifle.

The two blues stared blankly at their fallen comrade. Their expressions were almost identical in their disbelief.

His heart broke for the officer, but there was no time for anything but trying to save the rest of their lives. They might need some help with that.

"We can't help him now. You two need to keep your heads, got it?"

Slowly, one then the other nodded. Manny prayed they did. They had other problems.

"Marie! Marie, can you hear me?" he said.

Only the sound of unanswered static met his desperate plea.

Good God, were they all dead?

Before he could call her again, another deafening burst of hot metal ripped through the wall, striking about two feet lower than the previous volley, bullets ripping the table legs apart and lodging into the stove and refrigerator just inches above his head.

There was a time to analyze and a time to act.

If they wanted to live, they had to act.

He pointed at the two cops and motioned for them to raise their weapons, one at a lower level than the other.

They didn't have the luxury of trying to flank the shooter, so this would have to do.

Raising up, praying that the shooter would not fire again for another second or two, he aimed above the other two and began firing.

The two blues joined him as they raked the wall at three different levels before following his lead and diving back to the floor, already making every effort to reload their weapons.

An eerie, uncomfortable silence followed as he hugged the floor.

Had they hit him? Had they done better than that and taken the shooter out? Or was he waiting for them?

More silence.

As the silence lingered, Manny fixed his gaze on the dead young cop a few feet away. So young and so hopeful.

What the hell is wrong with this picture? Why is this senseless killing all he seemed to see anymore?

Gathering shaken wits, he didn't see any other choices left to him. There were five other officers on the other side of that wall somewhere, maybe still alive and possibly injured. He had to find out. There was no more time to waste.

Turning to the other two, he motioned for them to go out the back door and circle to the front of the house, one on each side of the house.

"What are you going to do?" mouthed one of the blues, his eye still wide.

Manny pointed to the door leading from the kitchen and motioned he was going through the door.

The second cop began to raise an objection; Manny waved it off.

"Go. One minute, then I'm in," he mouthed.

The two cops looked at each other and shrugged as if saying, "It's his ass." They checked their watches, and then hurried through the back door.

They could be right, Manny thought. *But I always knew I'd die being a cop.*

The faces of Jen and Ian rose up in his mind, then Chloe . . . then Louise.

He didn't want to die tonight, hardly. He wanted to grow old with Chloe and bounce a grandkid or two on his lap, watch them grow into fine young men and women. But what else could he do here?

People needed him to do what he had sworn he would do; protect the people from assholes like this one. There was no time to get angry or have doubts.

Glancing at his watch, he exhaled, rose to a crouch, and rushed the door.

He grabbed the knob, swung it open, and dove through, Glock poised and eyes wide open.

Two quick bursts of gunfire greeted his entrance.

The killer stood with his back to Manny, blood running down his left shoulder, pointing his automatic weapon at the front door, apparently shooting at the two cops Manny had sent out the back door.

That wasn't the whole scene.

There were four bloodied bodies of the Miami-Dade cops who had entered the front door scattered around the lit living room. His eyes searched for Marie.

He found her.

Marie Swifton's dark eyes were open, but her focus was on another world. The bullet that had taken away part of her forehead was the same culprit that sent her to the afterlife. Her hand rested on Duane James's back, their blood pooling together beneath them.

Without hesitation, Manny squeezed off three quick rounds.

He didn't need the last two.

The first bullet struck the shooter in the back of the head, dropping him to the floor, his rifle landing as he pitched forward into the flat-screen TV and then bounced back to the hardwood, facing Manny.

Rising quickly, Manny kept his gun leveled on the shooter until he realized the man had breathed his last. He stared at the face and, through the distorted features caused by his slug, recognized Eric Tovant.

In the next instance, the screen door burst open and the two cops entered, both yelling for the unsub to drop his weapon. It took a second for them to focus, but when they did, their pained revulsion seemed to embrace the entire room.

The first officer who had entered the door slowly dropped his weapon to his side then knelt beside one of the slain cops, tears rolling uncontrollable down to his chin.

"I'm sorry, Jake. We didn't know either, man. We didn't know, brother. I'm so sorry. Partners are supposed to have each other's backs. I'm so . . ."

The young man quit speaking then sat down cross-legged, putting his hand on his partner's chest, patting it slowly. The second officer swore, then hurried out the front door. The cop's dinner welled and splattered on the stoop while he petitioned God for help.

Manny shifted his attention to the four dead cops, blood covering half of the room. His mind had gown past the anger and dipped into the hopeless.

So this was it? This was what they got for being good cops? For trying to stand up for what was good? For trying to make the world a safer place?

Maybe Sophie was right. Maybe there was another life out there that would let them sleep at night and not be exposed to this kind of carnage. Was this life truly worth the price? And what if she lost Dean in this supposed noble arena? Was anything worth that?

The fifth body in this death-hole room begged his attention again. He tilted his head and gave it to him.

They had taken out Eric Tovant, and he wouldn't harm another soul, small consolation for the families of these brave cops.

With a great deal of effort, he pulled out his cell and dialed 911.

After giving the dispatcher the address, he hung up. Manny patted the young cop on the shoulder, still sitting by his fallen partner. Then he walked over to Marie, reached down, and gently closed her eyes for the final time.

CHAPTER-38

Stepping through the hospital door, Manny didn't wait for the elevator and hurried up the three flight of steps to the ICU floor where Sophie had texted him to come.

His lack of love for technology was obvious, but in this instance, he was glad for it. He didn't want to hear Sophie's voice. The last thing he needed after leaving that house of death was another bout with his emotions.

That was probably true with her after he had texted her first, telling her that Eric Tovant was dead, but that they had lost five cops ridding the world of Valentino.

Turning the corner and then continuing to room 3012, Manny felt his heart racing, and not just because of news regarding Dean, which was plenty emotional enough. He was sapped. Wired out. He felt like a fish at the end of its struggle to free itself from the hook and return to the water.

In all of his years as a cop, he'd never felt less control over his job, the unsubs, and above all, himself. Being strong, able to compartmentalize and concentrate on a killer's traits and personality had been what he'd been made for, or at least he used to think so. Now that self-assured mindset was suffering a major toll here in Miami. Then again, breaking a petty crook's ankle wasn't exactly in line with who he was either.

Forever, he would wonder if he should have guessed Eric Tovant's next move. Yet he had fully agreed with Marie, if not by his words, then by his actions. Five cops were dead because of it.

Five cops. Five cops chalked up to Valentino.

He prayed it wouldn't be six.

Manny found the room and reached out and touched the numbers as if to confirm them by touch, not truly trusting his eyes. The wooden double-door was closed, hiding the room's secrets from the outside world, from him.

Taking a deep breath, he turned the handle and stepped through.

Josh, Belle, and Sophie stood a few feet away from the man hooked to a billion wires and tubes on the bed. The smell of hospital disinfectant brushed his nose, the rhythmic actions of the ventilator pump the only sound in the room.

Belle held Sophie's hand while Josh stood so close to her that air would have trouble getting between them.

Sophie turned to Manny and tilted her head, offering a thin smile. There were no tears, no countenance of anger, pain, or signs of a pending emotional explosion or meltdown. She was more in control than he, it seemed.

"He's not dead," she said.

"Thank God," said Manny.

He made no attempt to disguise his relief. His knees felt a little weak at the release of emotion, but a burden had been lifted for now.

"Maybe. The doctors think if he makes it through the night that he'll have a chance," she said, still missing any real Sophie Lee emotion.

"He's tough and strong, he'll make it," said Josh.

"He will," said Belle.

Sophie nodded then slowly shuffled to Dean's side, bent and kissed him on the forehead, whispered something to him, kissed him again, and backed up to the other three.

"Let's go to the private waiting room," said Sophie. "I can't stay here and just watch whether he makes it or not. I have to get my mind off him or I'll go insane. Besides, I found out a couple things about Eric Tovant you need to know."

"Are you sure? That can wait. He's dead. Valentino won't hurt anyone else," said Manny.

"Yes, I'm sure. I don't care what the experts say, sitting here won't help either one of us. Not this time. I told Dean that, and he gets it. I know he gets it. As far as Eric Tovant and Valentino being one and the same, you'll have to decide that yourselves."

"What? Why?" asked Manny.

"Follow me."

He fell in line behind her with Josh and Belle behind him.

Manny had no idea what she was about to show them, but any sense of relief he'd felt moments ago had been obliterated. Yet, he wasn't surprised. He suspected something was not quite right, didn't he? But he was hoping against hope Eric Tovant's death was the end of this case. He was about to find out.

Sophie led them through the door to the room, stopping at the nurse's desk to tell them she'd be in the waiting room. She then continued through two more sets of doors into a secluded room. On top of the small rectangular table were three stacks of papers in various states of disarray piled around the laptop Manny had given Sophie.

She sat down in the chair as Josh, Belle, and Manny formed an arc facing her.

"I was going to show this to Belle and Josh when they got back a couple of hours ago, but then you texted me at about the same time the doctors came out of the OR—"

She bit her lip, then stuck it out in determination.

"Anyway, I thought you were just giving me busy work to keep my mind off from shit, but I thought I'd check this stuff out anyway. Most of that cross-referencing junk, you know, the locations of the murders and all of that, didn't lead to anything concrete until I finally got the profile on Eric Tovant."

She reached for a piece of paper with what Manny recognized as her handwriting.

"This piece of work has been nothing but trouble since he was about twelve. He has a juvie record longer than my arm, for starters. And that's just what I can find. Who knows what is still sealed away somewhere?

"His dad kept bailing his ass out of trouble, but in the late summer of 1995, the year Belle's friend was killed, daddy committed him to a private juvenile mental health facility in Gainesville."

"How long?" asked Manny.

"Now that's the golden question. It looks like he was there for three years because of school archives, but he has no official record of leaving the facility until the year 2000 when he turned eighteen."

"I don't get it," said Josh.

"I didn't either at first. It was confusing as hell because I found records where an Eric Tovant was enrolled in high school right here in Miami at age sixteen and graduated in the same year he was supposedly released from the institution."

"There could have been more than one Eric Tovant, right?' asked Belle.

"I checked that, and oddly enough, there were only two ever registered in any public record I could find. The first one would be about a hundred twenty years old today. The other would be around thirty-four."

"That's our guy then," said Josh.

"Maybe. Valentino has serious art ability, as warped as it is, right? But the canvassing report Marie had her people do with the colleges and art schools gave us nothing regarding an Eric Tovant. He didn't show up on the list of people who might have some interest in odd forms.

"I also found out, with the help of Kristen from the Miami-Dade Research Department, that he does not show up as registered in any college in Florida or any other college in the country."

"Did you find anything at all?" asked Belle.

"Yeah, maybe. His name came up associated with a bipolar/schizophrenia therapy group who had been making progress in treating their conditions about six years ago and then with some dumbass, radical militia faction in Georgia. The only other thing I found with a public record was the house he owned. It looks like someone, probably daddy, paid cash for it in 2003. There was no job info on him either."

"From what Belle and I found out about the family, Eric was probably on some kind of trust fund income," said Josh.

"Makes sense. We found one savings account in his name with an eighty-thousand-dollar balance. That's it, other than the two arrests for assault that he did a few days in jail for."

"What kind of assault?" asked Manny.

"He pistol-whipped some gangbanger during a fight in a bar, and he beat the hell out of a professor in some park down in South Beach."

Manny ran his hand through his hair. He was trying to make sense of what Sophie had shared so far, and it was brewing too slowly to suit his needs. None of this fit with Eric Tovant and Valentino being the same man. But that didn't mean they weren't, or hadn't been.

Schizophrenia in rare sub-forms could account for the dead man's behavior. God knew he'd seen that more than once. But that didn't feel right here. There was something else going on. Then it came together for him.

"Pictures? Did you find pictures of him?" asked Manny.

She nodded. "I found one, other than his mug shot, and was looking for more when I got interrupted by another report coming into me. I'll show you what I found in a second, but I have to tell you about the report first."

"Which report?" asked Belle.

"The preliminary forensic information from the warehouse. There are two things that yell at me, at least that I see."

"Let's hear it," said Manny.

"They found a lighter near the exit where he left the building and ran the prints against IAFIS. No match came up."

"How did they know that it belonged to the killer?" asked Josh.

"Good question," said Sophie, glancing at the door. "Luckily there were a couple smears of blood on the lighter and the word LOVER engraved on the bottom of it."

"So whoever owns that lighter is our killer?" asked Josh.

"It looks like it. The blood the CSU collected at the warehouse matched the drops on the lighter, but the DNA results didn't show up in CODIS."

"But it could still be Tovant," said Belle.

"It couldn't, actually," said Manny. "Unless there was the worst mix up of recordkeeping ever known to the FBI's database."

"Why?" asked Belle.

"He was arrested, twice. They would have had his fingerprints along with his DNA on file," said Manny.

"That makes no sense," said Belle, her calm demeanor unraveling some. "The cops in Saint Kitts said it was Eric Tovant who killed Cammy, and Valentino's MO is all over that murder."

"It is if the killer was actually Tovant."

"Pictures, Sophie?"

She pulled her eyes away from the door and looked at Manny.

"What? Oh yeah."

She hit the keys and then turned the laptop around.

"Here is the first picture I found."

Manny looked it up and down. The face was a bit younger and his hair longer, but the image was a dead ringer for the mugshot of the man known as Eric Tovant. The murderer he'd shot in the head.

"Okay. That's him. That's the man whose ass is now in the morgue," said Manny.

He caught the side glance from Josh, but didn't care. He was glad that Tovant was in that drawer. His only regret was that he hadn't got to him before he killed five cops.

"Belle. Does this look like the boy you saw in Saint Kitts?"

Exhaling, Belle stared at the face. She finally threw up her hands, exasperated.

"I only saw those eyes because of that damn scarf. I don't know. I mean this one looks crazy, with those wide peepers, but I just can't say for sure. I only remember how crazy he didn't look. So in control."

"Fair answer," said Manny. "What else do you have?"

"Hit the escape button. The next picture is the one I just found," said Sophie.

Manny tapped the button and a faded photograph of two young men, maybe in their early twenties, came into view.

Tall palm trees framed the young men as they stood in white sand, the blue-green ocean in front of a large boat as backdrop. They were both smiling, arms around each other's shoulders.

The young man on the left had sandy hair, a slighter build, and stood shorter than the one on the left, who was obviously Tovant. Ten years or so younger, but there certainly was no denying that it was him in the image.

"That's him on the left," said Josh.

"It is," said Manny.

"They look like buds," said Belle.

"They do. So where does someone with Tovant's problems find someone who he trusts enough to put his arm around? Paranoia is paranoia, and it would take a special bond for him to consent to a picture like this, in my opinion," said Manny. "Sophie, what do you think?"

She didn't answer right away. Once again, Sophie was lost in her thoughts, more likely her fears, her eyes fixed on the door. Manny touched her hand to get her attention.

"Go ahead, Sophie. Go be with Dean. We've got this," said Manny.

She hesitated, then shook her head.

"It will rip me a new one watching whatever happens with him. God in heaven, I love him, but I ain't watching him die on me. I can't do that."

"If you change your mind, we get it, okay?" said Manny.

He was doing his best to stay compartmentalized, but the walls were crumbling as the idea of what she was experiencing tugged at his heart.

Sophie cleared her throat. "Like anything on this planet could stop me, if I wanted to do that."

"That's true," said Josh.

Changing the subject, Manny pointed to the screen.

"Do you know where this picture came from? Do we know who this other kid is? Can we find out? Someone had to post that picture from somewhere. Facebook? Twitter? Ancestry.com or maybe some family webpage?"

"I don't know for sure. Dean and Alex are better geeks than I am when it comes to going deep into stuff like that, but let me see. All I know for now is that it came from a place called PhotoPail, and the source isn't always shown in the HTTP address or even on the display itself. Let me see if I can back into the source."

There was a sudden vibration in Manny's pocket. Then three separate ring tones as Sophie, Josh, and Belle all were received inbound calls at the same time.

His gut twisted. Even in this age of cell phones, he'd never heard all of them entertain a notification at the same time.

Pulling his phone out of his pocket, he realized he'd been wrong. It wasn't a call at all, but a text. Looking at the others, he saw that they had not received calls either. He read the text, expecting something, anything, far different than what he was about to read.

Agents. I wanted you to be the first to see my work, my labor of love, if you will. I tried to be discreet at first, to let these magnificent people be the stars of their own show, but, as usual, you law enforcement types have now made that an impossibility, insulting me in the process. The world has a right to see these people at their finest hour, and I'm going to make sure that happens.

Of course, the public will get to meet the creator of this eternal work as well, something that I resisted at first, but I realized, in the end, it would be impossible for Valentino to stay in the shadows. Touch the link below if you want to see what I've done to those who deserve an eternity of recognition before I release it to the masses. You'll have three minutes.

Manny scrolled further, not quite believing what he was seeing.

Oh, by the way, I see you've killed Eric. Too bad. He was a bit erratic and maybe you did him a favor. He'll receive a certain amount of fame for what he did and how he lived. That's all we can ask. Still, he was family, and you didn't have the right to take away family. Only I can do that. We will discuss that when the time comes, Agent Williams.

Enjoy the creations. I do.
Valentino.

The stunned silence was finally broken when Sophie stood and handed her phone to Manny.

"You know what? I can't do this right now. I'd rather be with Dean, even if he dies in my lap than to see what's on that link and then try to figure out why Tovant isn't Valentino."

CHAPTER-39

"The government? My wife? And why aren't you rotting your big ass away with some new boyfriend in a federal prison? This is the last time I ask before I do something stupid: what the hell is going on here?" asked Alex. "And I want the freaking truth. How can you be a spy or some shit and I never knew?"

Barb stood, bent toward him, placed her hand on his chest, and then spoke into his ear.

"If you'll be quiet, we'll explain the rest, okay?"

Licking his lips, Alex decided that she was right on that part. He needed to shut up and listen. Then, when he awoke from this dream, the drugs fully worn off, he'd be back in the room at Walter Reed.

The idea that he'd been married to this woman for a dozen years and never had a clue she was living some kind of double life was insane. Yet, here they were, maybe. Drugs. It had to be pain medication.

"First ting, mon. I can see what you be tinkin'. You not be dreamin' or under da influence of narcotics. Dis is all real, so get dat notion from yer mind."

So much for the dream idea.

"Dis is complicated, so I'll try to make it simple."

"It would help if you drop that dumbass accent. I've heard it come and go, and right now I'd like it to go," said Alex.

"I'll do my best, but it is in der when I don't think about it."

"Better."

"All right, mon," said Braxton smiling.

"Funny."

"Seven years ago, der was a special outfit formed to oversee three other establishments. The top cats in each organization, DEA, CIA, and FBI, wanted more impartial accountability and it made sense to do dat. The idea wasn't to interfere, but to address situations that seemed like they were becoming out of control."

"Like what, for example?" asked Alex, his interest growing.

"Argyle's mind control experiments for one. The CIA's involvement in Africa and in Venezuela and the resources allocated to certain groups of rebels, and my favorite had to do wid the DEA agents taking huge bribes from the Mexican cartels. And before you ask, mon, yes, it happened and more than once."

"Wait, before you go any further, you told us you were a US Marshal and worked with the DEA and didn't get involved in espionage and that spy world shit," said Alex.

"I did, I just didn't tell you everything. You didn't need to know all of da dirty little secrets."

"So when Josh had you arrested, that was a ruse? You already knew each other? If you did, you fooled the hell out of all of us, even Manny."

"Yes, to both questions. In a twisted way, part of the deception was to keep me away from Manny before he finished putting together what he would eventually figure out. I know that I'm not telling you anything you don't know, no doubt dat, but I have never seen the likes of that man. He would have been a hell of a deep undercover agent."

"Go on," said Alex.

He was trying his level best to not look at his wife, but he felt her eyes on him, no doubt reading like she had always done.

Always.

"The second reason for having me arrested in such a public way was to make sure that the three agencies would believe that no one was untouchable when it came to breaking the rules. Which it appeared I did by conspiring to commit murder, a huge no-no for our group. The pretend arrest allowed me to dig deeper into something that needed to be investigated in a less than orthodox way. I'm not going to go into that here, but that cover allowed us to discover what was truly going on with some of dat prosthetic research."

"Which was?"

The giant of a man dabbed at his perspiring forehead, giving him that Mister Clean look, enhanced by his gold earrings and that sudden, gleaming white grin.

"Barb?" asked Braxton, motioning toward his wife.

At first, Alex didn't look at her, balancing his indescribable love for her against the realization that she had been living another life.

Usually that particular nuance was reserved for men whose wives gradually discover that their hidden fears were a reality. That their knight in shining armor had three other wives or was a serial killer rapist who doubled as a mild-mannered accountant and dedicated family man. Not for men who worked as cops and thought their wives were staying at home, doing charity work, and visiting their mothers or some other normal function.

He felt her long, warm fingers caress his cheek and was powerless to resist. He turned in her direction.

"Weapons research, Alex," she said. "Your new hand will do all that the research says it will, giving you the best bio technology of its kind on earth. It can do all that it's designed to do. What the brochure didn't say, so to speak, was that the circuitry could also be modified, with just a few tweaks, to add some seriously dangerous weaponry."

"What? Like what and how would they do that? I think I would know if there was some super sophisticated automatic laser gun or whatever, attached to my damned hand."

"Way too many cyborg movies for you," she said. "It wouldn't be that obvious, of course. It would be more like a concentration of some germ-warfare agent or even a small dirty bomb. Whatever the situation would call for at the time. All they would have to do is call you in to the hospital for a systems check or an upgrade and set it up."

"Who in the hell is *they*?" asked Alex.

"That's a billion-dollar mystery, of sorts. When you and Josh went to Vegas, I went to a designated meeting with an informant, supposedly, to find out more about who is paying these doctors exorbitant amounts of money to install the circuitry and software that makes your hand more than a prosthetic limb. It didn't go well, and the woman was dead when I got there. We've had nothing but dead ends since. We're hoping that a couple of our associates can help loosen the tongue of your two surgeons, but we suspect that will be a dead end too."

"Wait, you're interrogating two world-renowned surgeons to see who might be behind something that I'm having a hard time believing is even true?"

"It don't matter what you believe, Alex. It only matters that we know the truth," said Braxton.

"He's right, Alex."

"It sounds like paranoia to me."

"It's not. At any rate, we know the brains behind this is someone employed by one of the three agencies. We suspect someone high up, but we haven't been able to track that individual down."

"That's just freaking crazy. How would arming me with a weapon work exactly? I work for the BAU and do forensic work. Using me, and killing my fat ass in the process, makes no sense."

"It would totally depend on the desired effect. You travel all over the country and then some. Plus, you're a Fed. That makes you a perfect candidate for this kind of manipulation."

Alex's head spun with the sudden change in his fortunes, not to mention his wife's involvement in all of this. These two believed what they were saying. Braxton as a fruitcake was one thing, but his wife? No matter how hard he wanted to believe this was just some fabrication, he was losing the battle. They were right on one thing. If someone could really pull the strings Barb and Braxton were saying they could and would have a reason to use him for some horrifying attack, he, with his FBI credentials, could get into places most could not.

He laid his head back, considering his next step. It came to him. He looked to his beautiful wife, who had somehow become even sexier.

"I need for you to tell me in what situation this weapon thing could be used, and I need proof. I'm a damned scientist, for crying out loud."

"I can do both," she said.

Her confidence in her answer caused a shiver to spider down his spine. The last of his doubtful resolve was evaporating quickly.

"You were in Ireland a couple of years ago, then San Juan, and we just got back from Mexico, right?"

He nodded.

"What if, for some ungodly reason, this individual, if it is an individual, wanted to stir up trouble between two factions that were always in tension status? God knows there are dozens of those to choose from. What if they wanted to start a war by killing a group of leaders or unleashing some chemical or germ agent and then spin it so it was the other side's doing?"

"That sounds out there. And why?"

"Why is always a good question, usually money or a power spin that leads to money. As for out there, really? How about Bosnia? Or maybe Rwanda and the genocide of hundreds of thousands of innocents. Or maybe Somalia. Hell, let's not even mention the Middle East and Iraq and Iran. Do you think that those conflicts evolved on their own momentum?"

No. No, he didn't.

"I can continue all night, but you love empirical, measurable evidence so let me give it to you."

She nodded to the first man who'd entered the room with her, and he walked around Alex's left while snapping on blue rubber gloves.

With dexterity Alex wouldn't have thought possible for a man that size, he bent toward the machine stabilizing his arm. In a few seconds, he had removed three of the long pins and lifted a small metal plate from the backside of Alex's wrist or forearm—Alex wasn't sure which because that side of his arm was hidden from his view.

The man held the plate out to Alex. He exhaled, then reached over with his right hand and took it.

"Read the print on the lower left of that plate," said Barb.

Holding the plate higher to get more light exposure, he squinted to read the fine print.

NOT TO EXCEED SIXTEEN OUNCES. OVERLOAD COULD CAUSE FUNCTIONAL DAMAGE.

"So?"

"That is the cover for a tiny compartment that can be filled with anything from plutonium to Ebola."

"That's what you say."

"If I'm lying, then why would there be an empty compartment in an area under your arm?

In all of your research and the information Josh provided to you, did you see any prototypes with that particular feature? How would that fit into an efficient design?"

She had him there. He and Dean had even stayed up late one night, going over the specs and how well the prosthesis had been designed to look like his wrist and forearm, in size at least.

The man took the plate from Alex's hand, replaced it, and then moved back to the door where he'd been standing.

Alex let all that he'd just heard and read sink in further. He figuratively placed himself in the context of a crime scene and mulled the facts and evidence that could lead to some definitive conclusions. It helped him to mentally go to a place that could help him sort out what he'd been told.

Action, however, was far better than words.

Barb and Braxton had brought him here, at probably great risk to all involved. They obviously had some forethought into what they would have to do after the surgery and prepared this room. Why do all of that? It sure as hell wasn't some practical joke or elaborate kidnap attempt. Who would want to kidnap him anyway? Surely not his wife. Again why?

And, now that he thought about it with less emotion, why had the government agreed to pay the whole amount for the new hand surgery and subsequent care without ever having a thought to turn it over to an insurance company? He'd thought it was because he lost the hand during an assignment, but government bean counters were never that generous.

He wasn't an expert on micro-expressions, face twitches, or eyes roaming down to someone's feet when they were lying, but he didn't get a sense of any of that from either of them, especially Barb.

The writing on the metal plate didn't lie. Although he couldn't see the area where that cover had come from, he'd never seen a piece like that in any of the schematics. She was right about that.

There was one more thing that needed to be addressed directly before he could decide to scream like a school girl or go along with this story that was sounding more and more plausible.

"How long have you been working for this special group?"

His wife's smile was as radiant and pure as ever.

"It's not that important, but I know you want to know. I was recruited out of college by the CIA. My scores on some random aptitude tests, which I thought were leading to something else entirely, were good enough to get a personal interview with the head of personnel with them."

"The CIA?"

"Yes. I trained as an inside analyst and then, a year before I met you, started to spend time in the field." Barb kissed him full on the lips. "After I fell in love with you, I tendered my resignation. I wanted to be married to you more than being involved in the work. I knew that sometimes the assignments could follow you home, literally, so I didn't want to endanger you. Or anyone close to you. The organization didn't want me to quit entirely so I worked random assignments that could only have certain types of endings."

"Let me guess, those sudden trips to your mother's or sister's?"

"Mostly. I did my job and came home, and I liked how that worked. I then met Braxton the year before Manny and he had their first encounter in the El Yunque rain forest.

"I gradually became a part of this overseer group, and that's how we got to this point."

"What do you mean certain types of endings?"

"Assignments I can't and won't discuss, okay? But I wouldn't waste any time thinking about them. Just know I did my job, like you do," she said.

Thinking about what she may or may not have been a part of could blow an already traumatized brain to pieces. He decided that conversation was for another time, if it ever happened. But one thing he knew for sure, because the evidence said so, this was no prank or pack of lies. His heart knew it better than his head—and that's something to admit for a science guy.

"So Josh is not only my boss, but has been watching over me closely, right?"

"Yes," said Braxton. "It was why he came to see you before Las Vegas and took you with him. You weren't there to simply help that investigation, but to get out of Walter Reed until we received more intel."

Alex raised his right hand in a frustrated gesture.

"Good God, I feel like I just fell into some screwed-up version of a Jason Bourne movie."

"Naw. Bourne has a cushy situation compared to dat ting we do," said Braxton with a full belly laugh.

For the first time since before surgery, Alex smiled. Then it vanished.

"Okay. So what now? Say I buy into all of this, what happens next?"

"You'll stay here until you have recovered and we can wrap up some loose ends. Then you'll go back to work like normal," said Barb.

"Normal?"

"Yes. We've screwed up your surgery as a viable weapon this time so you won't be in any future danger," she said.

"You're sure about that?"

"I am. The only danger you'll put yourself in is if you talk about this. You can't even say anything to Manny."

"How am I going to do that? We go way back."

"You just do it."

His wife sat back down beside him, touching him again. "People could die and probably would, if you can't keep this under your hat. Even to Manny."

"It won't be that easy. He's going to think something's up after this case is over and he comes to visit and I'm not at Walter Reed. So will Sophie."

His apparent saviors looked at each other, then Braxton spoke. His voice much quieter.

"They have a couple problems of their own right now. Josh will handle tings on his end accordingly."

It would have been impossible for Alex to hide the distress he felt at Braxton's words.

"What the hell does that mean? Are they in trouble?"

"They'll be fine. You just need to concentrate on your recovery," said Braxton.

"Yeah, like that will be a walk in the park," said Alex, meeting the big man's eyes.

"We'll help," said Barb.

Alex felt a prick on his arm and turned to his wife.

"Really? You did that again?"

Then he was out.

CHAPTER-40

Manny watched as the door closed behind Sophie. He took three steps after her then stopped, squeezing his phone so hard that he thought it might break into pieces, not that that would bother him. Valentino's communication was just another reason to hate wireless signals that can and do reach anyone, wanted or not. At that moment, he couldn't think of a time when that idea was less wanted.

Did his partner need him more than they needed to unravel who Valentino was and stop him? Hell, a better question was: did Sophie want him around? This fight for Dean's life was far more personal than most people from outside the struggle to comprehend it could realize, something he completely understood.

Other than Jen, and that wasn't an all-of-the-time, every-moment kind of thing, he wanted to see no one or be with anyone immediately after

Louise had died. But everyone was different, and his friend might be the opposite.

"Manny. We need to find this freak," said Josh softly.

"I know, damn it, I know. I'll be back."

He hurried through both doors and turned the corner toward Dean's room. Sophie stood there waiting for him. By the look on her face and her folded arms, she'd known he would come after.

She took both of his hands. "I love that you are you, Manny. And I know what you're thinking, but I need to be alone with him. We have things to talk about, our personal stuff."

"I get it. I just want you to know that catching Valentino isn't as important to me as being here for you. Not now. A few hours ago, yes, but not now. I—"

"You don't need my blessing or some shit, Manny. I know you've had a rough few months . . . hell, a rough three years and we've all died a little with you, just like you're dying with me right now.

"We talk about this job ripping out what's left of our souls, but you need to get it together and find this guy. You have to find out who Valentino is and why Tovant shot five cops and didn't seem to mind dying for it. No one else is going to be as much help figuring that out. I sure as shit ain't going to be any good."

"But—"

She squeezed his hands.

"Stop. Listen to me. You also know damn well that Valentino's not done. More people are going to check out if you don't get to work. I just can't help right now."

She reached up and kissed him on the cheek.

"Do what you do and let me do what I have to, okay?"

Then Sophie turned and disappeared into the ICU room that held her and Dean's fate.

He ran his hand through his hair, fixed on the door Sophie had entered, then turned back to the office where Belle and Josh waited.

"Are you good?" asked Josh.

"No, but Sophie set me straight. We need to get to work."

"We do," said Belle. "I'm so confused right now."

"There's some of that going around," said Josh.

Manny nodded, then pointed to the laptop.

"Belle, you're probably better at some of this computer stuff than Josh and I are. So if you don't mind?"

"We'll see," she said as she sat down in front of it.

"Before we explore this link, we need to get our cyber people involved. If this can be traced, they'll be able to do it," said Manny.

"Already taken care of, Manny," said Josh. "I sent the link to Quantico as well as to the local office. The South Florida office apparently has one of the best hacker types on the planet on staff, and we want them involved."

"How did you know about the hacker?" asked Manny.

"Hey, I can still surprise you once in a while. Besides, the people in HQ told me about her. I also have twelve FBI agents on the ready, along with over fifty Miami-Dade cops. All prepared to move in an instant."

"Fair enough. I guess it helps to be the boss over the BAU."

"I have some privileges," said Josh, his face growing more somber. "The cyber folks are ready to move and open the site in ways I've never heard of when I give the ready. They're waiting on us to see what we see first."

"We're probably going to need that," said Manny.

"Will you answer a question before we do this? It could be important," said Josh.

"If I can," said Manny.

"What happened at the house, exactly? I liked Marie. She and her people were good cops."

That was a good question, wasn't it? What had really happened there?

In the rush of simply trying to stay alive, then his shooting of Tovant, and the crazy-ass aftermath of that nightmarish slaughter accompanied with getting the locals educated on what had happened in real-time, then receiving

Sophie's text . . . he hadn't thought a lot about the whys.

"Tovant certainly had a vicious past. After you sent us his name and we checked into his background, we knew that going in. We also assumed he was probably Valentino because of what the island cops told you. Hell, the timing was even right for him to be on the run after Valentino had left the warehouse and Sophie and I found Dean. We didn't truly believe he would come back to his house. That didn't fit with this man's level of intelligence.

"Everything had just sort of snapped into place, and we thought his arrogance had put him in deep trouble. We assumed we'd find an empty house and be able to go over it with a fine-tooth comb for leads, especially since there seemed to be no one around," said Manny.

"Whose idea was it to go in?" asked Josh.

"Marie had the final say. We both thought it felt bad, but she went ahead anyway. That's when the shooting started."

Manny exhaled, hoping the images and sounds of that would vanish. They didn't. They never would.

"The forensic people are going over the house now, but I don't think it'll do any good," said Manny.

"Why?" asked Belle.

"Tovant isn't Valentino, obviously. So that means Valentino was probably never in that house. And if he had been, he's too smart to leave any traces. They'll probably only find more evidence of Tovant's violent nature."

"If that's true, then what's the connection between these two? The Saint Kitts people were sure it was him and that his father took care of cleaning up the mess of Cammy's murder," said Belle.

"I don't know. It's like we were led down this path but not quite, if that makes sense."

"Not really, but I sort of get what you mean," said Belle. "Things fit, but then they don't."

"There seems to be only one way to find out and dig deeper. Open the link," said Manny.

They moved behind Belle and watched in silence as she typed in the HTTP address.

Josh had his hand on the send button on his phone, ready to alert the two cyber agents when it was okay to climb into the site.

She looked up at Manny, her big, dark eyes filled with anxiety.

"Do it," he whispered.

She did as Josh sent the okay.

The screen jumped to life revealing the devil in his most perverted of perversions. It was all Manny could do to keep his composure and try to do what profilers do.

On the top of the webpage, in each corner, was a cluster of pink hearts pierced with red arrows. Between the hearts was the word VALENTINO in the same Algerian style of type he'd used to carve his name into his victim's heads and chests.

The site was running in real time, quartered off into equal sections.

The top two panels revealed explicit images of the first two crime scenes, a new picture scrolling every few seconds in perfect sync with each other. The young couple was still bound to the tree, the photos, showing various body parts and the perfect circles carved in place.

The second panel showed the same systematic display involving the Blankses, only about a five-second delay, allowing for the viewer to see the images for that long before the next one scrolled in.

"My God," whispered Belle.

As horrific as that was, the show really began as the bottom two panels, which were previously dark, sprang to life revealing two more sets of victims.

The one on the lower left began scrolling first but at a slower pace than the top two panels. Valentino wanted to make sure they were getting a good look at the new victims that law enforcement had yet to discover.

Two African Americans, a man and a woman, were lying stretched out, hands over their heads, bound with duct tape, dressed in only their undergarments, on what appeared a large living room floor that had once been covered with white or cream-colored carpet. The blood from their injuries had turned most of it to a sickening scarlet.

The second picture flashed, and Manny could see the gunshot wounds running down both sides of each body, but Valentino had been careful to not hit any main arteries or their hearts, as far as he could tell.

The next picture revealed a close up of each of them. The distinctive white triangles covering parts of their upper bodies made for a horrific scene against their dark bodies. It was as if he'd used some chemical to bleach or burn them into existence. VALENTINO was once again carved or burned into their chests and foreheads . . . with a new twist.

On both victims, just below Valentino's name, rested what appeared to be Miami-Dade police badges.

The sudden surge of sound startled him.

"More eternal art to come. Be patient my lovelies. These six deserved to be immortalized as do the next two. I love them enough to give them that," came Valentino's voice through the computer.

Then the fourth panel came to life, showing a row of triangles in rainbow-like colors, ending with more heart clusters running the full-length of that section.

Pure evil. Manny's heart skipped a beat. Then instead of fear, he felt that ever-increasing anger reappear. He'd kill Valentino with his bare hands if he could only touch him.

Shut it down, Williams. No emotion. Shut it down, for now.

He did.

"Josh. Anything from our cyber people?"

His boss had turned away and was already on the phone.

Belle had shut the top of the laptop, but he could see her wheels turning.

Good girl.

"Listen. I need to know what's going on," said Josh. "No bullshit, just information I can use. Got it?"

He kept the phone to his ear for a few more moments.

"Damn it. Keep working," he said. Then he hung up.

"They can't trace this, but are still trying. Apparently he's using a proxy IP address program that bounces the source of the signal all over the world at four-second intervals. One second the source is in California, four seconds later, it's in Iceland. You get the picture. Not to mention that the IP address can really only put us in the general vicinity of the source, so we can't truly pinpoint the ass hat without getting lucky," said Josh, shaking his head.

"Great. What else?" asked Manny.

Josh rubbed his face with both hands. "This link recognition protocol has been screwed up from the beginning. One of those cyber experts should have thought of this. Just for once, I'd like to be the dog here; I'm tired of being the fire hydrant. I don't know how this shit works, and I wish someone would have warned us that this could happen."

"What could happen?" asked Manny.

"It looks like when we accessed the link, we released the website into the general public by some Internet trigger program. Right about now, there are millions of people on the planet that are getting this site shipped into their email queues. Every one of those people have the potential to meet the Valentino family. Shit. I need a drink."

"So we can't trace him, he's killed again, we have no idea where he killed them, and the victims could be cops. On top of that, his victims are going to be famous in a way that they'd never dreamed, plus he's getting ready to do it again in, oh, about. . . ." said Manny looking at his watch, "five hours, if he's sticking with his timetable and accelerating his killing by twelve-hour increments . . . and we can't seem to find him."

"Throw in Dean fighting for his life and five dead cops and we've screwed the pooch like no other day I can remember. I don't have a clue where to go next," said Josh.

Manny was ready to respond, but the thundering epiphany storming his brain wouldn't allow it.

Pulse racing, he thought about something Josh had said regarding family. Valentino had mentioned Tovant as family in his text, and he knew from experience that most people have more than one type of family. Work, friend, and play family often became more important than blood family.

He considered what exactly family could mean to someone like Valentino versus someone liked Tovant as the second picture of the two young men came to mind.

Closing his eyes, he drew on something he'd seen a long time ago in another case file. Could that be it? Could what he suspected be true?

His whole professional life had depended on these revelation moments. Most of the time, he was right.

"Belle, can you show me that picture of the two young men again?"

She looked at him, recognizing the underlying excitement in his voice.

"Yeah, that one's right here. We didn't close out of the webpage where Sophie found it."

The picture filled the screen again as Manny focused on two details that he'd missed. He wanted to slap his forehead. Maybe new cops, or lazy ones, would miss these things, but how could four seasoned detectives?

Then again, he supposed he knew how. They had been worrying about their own people and not concentrating on their job. Maybe that's how it was supposed to be.

He'd dwell more on that later. He felt like they were back on the road to finding Valentino, so "personal needs" were once again placed on the back burner.

"Belle. I need three things. We were interrupted after I asked if we could find out where that second picture came from and if we could ID the second kid in the picture."

"Yes, we were. And our heads went straight up our rectums when we got Valentino's text," said Belle.

"Well said. Please send that picture to the lab in Quantico. I want them to run that through the new facial recognition software the Bureau just spent a ton of money on to see if they can find a match in the database. They'll have to age him about ten years or so, but we might get lucky."

"Okay."

Belle saved the image to the desktop, opened up her secure government email account, and then sent it to the supervisor in charge of forensic imaging.

"Do you think this kid is important here? Maybe even Valentino?" asked Josh.

"I don't know. It's probably a long shot. But if we can ID him, maybe that will lead to another lead because he may know more about Tovant than we do," said Manny.

"That's worth a shot," said Belle. "What else?"

Manny pointed to the top of the computer screen.

"If you look at the very top right corner, you can see what looks like a partial image of an American flag."

Belle leaned closer to the screen, squinting.

"Oh, hey I see it. Good eyes, Manny."

"We know the boat is from the US and you can see a row of registration numbers running along the bow. Can you blow up the center of that photo enough to see the boat's registration numbers?"

"Yeah, that's pretty basic. There are a few programs that can bring photos like that into focus. Boats are registered by state, so it might take a while, but we'll start with the Southern states and go from there. I'll start on that in a minute. You said there were three things."

"Yes I did. This one is obvious, but we need to do it anyway."

"It seems to me that the Tovant family, with their business and social status, should have more than their fair share of pictures available on the web. Can you do a search to find what's out there? According to the Saint Kitts cops, Eric was a single child. I want to see the happy family, if we can."

"Crap. That's another one of those 'well, duh's.'"

"Not necessarily," said Josh. "Why would you care about that? I mean we have his picture right here."

"Just a hunch. These two look like friends a while. We don't know how long. Life-long buddies? Just from high school? Bar-hopping friends? What? It will help establish the kind of friend this man is or was to Tovant and maybe lead to more information as well."

Josh stretched his neck one way, then the other, his eyes never leaving Manny's face.

"I know that tone in your voice, Williams. What are you really after here? You already know what Tovant looks like and we're in the process of running down this other young man, if we can. This seems like repetitive busy work to me, so spill it."

"It's a shot in the dark, okay? Back about nine years ago, when I was working a case in Lansing, I had to pass it off to Gavin to go to a seminar that our captain required all new detectives to attend. I'd gotten out of doing the seminar a couple times so I had no choice. So off to New York I went."

"Oh, I remember that one," said Belle.

Manny nodded. "It was the last thing I wanted to do. Anyway, I got assigned a case study that forced me to choose between potential perps who had become friends and were knocking off a liquor store. One of them then killed a store owner. Based on what we'd collected as evidence and some behavioral tendencies, we had to decide which of these punks would be a killer and which one probably couldn't go that far."

"And?" asked Josh.

"What we didn't know was that they were screwing with the NYPD and had switched IDs to confuse the investigation."

"Switched IDs with each other?" asked Josh.

"That's what we thought. But the kid who had actually done the killing stole a third ID from one of his friends and somehow had fake credentials created to further remove himself from being a suspect."

"Shit. You think Eric Tovant isn't really Eric Tovant?" asked Josh.

"Good God," said Belle.

Before Manny could answer, Josh's phone rang. He held up his hand for Manny to wait. After a few moments, Josh's eyes grew wider and exhibited the beginnings of a smile. A full minute passed before Josh spoke again.

"What? Really? That's unbelievable. Text me the address; we'll meet you there."

Josh hung up, but the wry smile grew.

"That was the captain who took over for Marie. Never mind all of that other stuff we were going to do. It seems that Manny was headed down the right path. We've got the son of a bitch. Let's go."

CHAPTER-41

"What the hell are you talking about?" asked Manny as they flew down the steps of the hospital.

The three of them reached the first floor, Belle doing her best to keep up, when Josh stopped to address Manny.

"We all know the saying that good police work is great, but a good lead solves cases."

"That's right," said Manny. "So?"

"So Valentino has apparently done himself in. One of the people who saw his feed through the emails announcing the website also happened to be someone who recognized the lettering of the word VALENTINO on one of the victim's foreheads."

"What?" asked Belle. "How?"

"The caller happened to be a supervisor at a local advertising company, Chase Advertising, to be exact. He said he was going through an employee's computer work files—an employee he thought strange and out there, by the way—

looking for a completed template for an ad campaign. He stumbled across a personal file that had this very same Algerian version of the word VALENTINO displayed on a logo graphic. He called 911 to report it, and now we have him identified."

Manny frowned. "Sound's great, but who is he?"

"You'll like this. His name is Benjamin Grimes. And guess where he spent his summers?"

"Saint Kitts?" asked Belle.

"She wins a Kewpie doll. It gets better. Apparently the Miami-Dade research folks found out that he spent time with the Tovant family, and they even paid for his education because his own family couldn't afford it."

"That probably explains the picture of both of them together. How did they find that out?" asked Manny.

Josh glanced at his phone, then looked up to Manny and Belle.

"I didn't ask and don't care. We've got the text with his address. Let's talk in the car. His house is about fifteen minutes away."

Once they were in the Bureau's SUV, Manny driving, it occurred to him that he needed to see something else.

"Josh, do we have a picture of Grimes?"

"I'll ask for one. But the locals are going to beat us there. We won't need one."

"Just get it."

Manny turned onto 95 and gunned it, lights flashing from the roof of the white SUV.

"Why do you need a picture?"

"I want to know who we're looking at, that's all."

A few minutes later, as they were approaching their exit, Josh handed Manny his phone.

"The JPEG is loading. Our boy will make an appearance shortly."

He glanced at the screen, then back to the road. It was taking too long to finally get a look at Valentino.

Pushing the brakes, Manny hit the exit ramp and then pulled off at the bottom near the stop sign, Josh's phone still in his hand.

"What are you doing?" asked Josh impatiently.

"I can't drive and try to watch for this picture to make an app—"

The screen lit up, interrupting Manny and subsequently framing Valentino.

The image showed an ordinary young man with traces of sandy blond hair and what appeared to be a slight frame. It didn't take facial recognition software to identify the young man in the photo. He was the second kid in the picture that Sophie had found of Tovant and Grimes.

He glanced at Josh then back to the picture on the phone.

The image of Valentino, and make no mistake this time, this man was their killer, raised a different emotion for Manny. Hate was never something he'd entertained, at least not in the true sense. Right now, at this minute, he hated Benjamin Grimes. There was no other way to describe it.

"Give me that phone. I want to see what this prick looks like."

Josh pulled the phone from Manny's hands and stared at the lighted screen, as Manny turned right and sped toward the house that belonged to Grimes.

"So this is him?" asked Josh. "He doesn't look like much."

Belle reached into the front seat and ripped Josh's phone from his hand.

Manny waited for her reaction.

It didn't take long.

"Damn it. That's him. Those eyes are the same. That's the guy who killed Cammy," said Belle, her emotion welling.

"Belle, are you sure?" said Manny.

"Yes. No mistaking that cocky gaze. I never thought I'd see him again."

There was a sense of relief in Belle's tone. Maybe she'd slayed at least one of her dragons by just knowing that this killer had been identified as the one who killed her friend all of those years ago.

He knew it would work for him.

After reaching the crossroads that was closest to Valentino's home, Manny turned down the street and had to slam on the brakes. There were at least ten cruisers and unmarked cars parked along both sides of the road, lights pulsing so brightly that the street looked like a noon-time party.

That total didn't count Miami-Dade's version of a SWAT vehicle that had already pulled up into the small front yard, its bright spotlight shining on the front door.

"So much for subtle," said Josh.

"I'm sure they did it right before they announced their presence. They, we, don't need any more dead cops," said Manny.

He parked the vehicle and they exited quickly. Manny led the way as they hurried toward the front of the house on the safe side of the street, careful to stay low behind the row of squad cars until they reached the man in charge.

Captain Howser, a tall man with a thick black mustache and gold-rimmed glasses tucked under his cap, held a bullhorn in his left hand as he crouched behind one of the green unmarked vehicles.

"Glad you Feds finally made it. But I think we have this one under control."

"We just want to watch him go down," said Manny.

"That's about to happen, so hang tight."

"Is he in there?" asked Josh.

"Our spotters say yes. The infrared heat scan verifies one person inside near the back of the house. We have four snipers set up. One in the back. One in the front, and one on each side. He won't be going anywhere but to jail or into the damned ground."

That was fine from where Manny stood. He thought Sophie would feel the same.

Howser then stood, still leaning over, then circled to the front of the vehicle, protected by an open car door. He switched on the bullhorn with a familiar screech Manny hadn't heard in years.

"Benjamin Grimes. This is the police. Come out with your hands raised. You won't be harmed if you surrender now. You have three minutes."

"That's not much time," said Belle. "They must not give a rat's ass if he comes out in one piece or not."

"Do you?" asked Manny, hearing the edge in his own voice.

She looked at him with a vein of curiosity.

"I didn't think so, but maybe. I'd like to ask him a few questions, then they can do whatever the hell they want to him."

"Either way, he's not going to come out of that house. My money says they'll have to go in and get him," said Josh.

Josh had no more then finished his sentence when his prediction proved to be wrong.

The front door swung open, slamming into the porch wall of the ranch, and stayed ajar.

A strained hush came over the sixty or so cops as each of them waited for Valentino to make another move. Manny was no exception, but he found himself standing taller so that he could see the front door even better.

With his right hand, he touched the Glock resting in his shoulder holster.

Each second seemed a century as the doorway remained open without Grimes exiting the house.

The first explosion broke the night's silence, putting Manny back on his haunches while he ducked for protection behind the squad car beside Josh and Belle. She was covering her ears, practically crawling inside Josh's shirt. Although he didn't want to be in Josh's shirt, anyplace that could insulate him more would have been fine.

Gunshots were one thing. He could handle that. Explosions reminiscent of wartime attacks were another. Noisy, far-reaching destruction wasn't on his list of enjoyable things.

After his ears stopped ringing, he looked over the car hood again at the house Valentino had destroyed.

The explosion had come from the back of the house. Flames were already jumping toward the roof in the middle of the home.

Just as cops up and down the row of cars began to show themselves, a second explosion, not as loud or as violent as the first, obliterated the windows in the front of the house and sent chards of debris flying over the SWAT vehicle.

This time, Manny stayed vertical, still watching the front door for any sign of Benjamin Grimes.

With each passing moment, the fire grew higher and more intense as the heat and the stench of burning wood and plastic began to filter through the already hot Miami air.

There was no question where the fate of this house was headed, and Captain Howser reacted accordingly, barking orders through his radio.

"Get these cars out of here and get that SWAT truck away from that yard and down the street. Pull all of our people back. We need to make room for the fire department's trucks. Then push these rubbernecks back to the next row of houses. We don't need this kind of aggravation turning into something worse. Move your asses, people."

The scramble of bodies and vehicles was almost immediate. Manny was no fire-scene expert, but this house didn't have long to go before it became a memory.

His eyes shifted back to the door, his frustration moving up step by step.

"Come on out you bastard. Come on," whispered Manny as he began to feel a portion of the heat coming from the house.

Don't be a damned coward. Come out and take your medicine.

The last thing Manny expected from someone like Valentino was a suicide attempt. It didn't fit his ideology. He had too much to show the world, in Manny's estimation, but it was beginning to look like he'd missed the mark on that part of Valentino's profile.

"He'll come out," said Belle, standing up beside Manny. "He won't kill himself."

"His profile says he'll come out," said Manny, doubting it more and more with each passing second.

"If he doesn't, it'll save the government a ton of money," said Josh.

Manny nodded. "It would, but then we don't get to watch him rot in his cell."

"That's true," said Josh.

Off to Manny's right, Captain Howser's radio began to fill with static, then the message came through the confusion loud and clear.

"Sir, this is SWAT Commander Briggs. We hear a man yelling for help from inside the house. What are your orders?"

"Help? Yelling for help?" asked Howser.

"Yes sir. Repeat: what should we do?"

Howser ran his hand over his face, his eyes darting to one side and then the other.

By now, the flames were reaching higher than ever. The back part of the house was quickly becoming a dangerous precursor to what was going to happen to the rest of it.

The captain looked at Josh.

"I know what protocol says, but what does the FBI think?"

Josh never hesitated.

"You can't endanger your men and women. Who knows, he may have one hell of a grand finale explosion waiting for whoever runs through that front door. And God knows, he's not worth taking the chance," said Josh.

"That's my thought. We've lost enough good people today."

Manny was ready to agree with them, but he suddenly couldn't. There was something off here. But what?

Yelling for help. Yelling for help.

That was it.

Howser was ready to respond when Manny grabbed his arm.

"Wait. Patch me into the commander."

"Why?"

"No time to waste. I want to hear the voice of the man asking for help."

"Why in hell do you want to do that?"

"Just do it."

"I would," said Josh. "He must have a good reason."

After a few more seconds, Howser shrugged.

"Okay."

Fifteen seconds later, a SWAT member moved a few feet closer to the front of the house carrying a large transparent cone used to amplify sound. He then raised his hand to signal he was ready.

"Here it comes, Agent," said the commander.

At first, Manny heard nothing, then he heard everything. Above all of the racket was a voice crying out in unmistakable pain and terror.

"Help me. I need help. I can't get free. Help me."

The voice was deep, even in panic mode. There was also a trace of Latino dialect in the way he finished his words. He waited.

The man trapped inside repeated himself again, more angst than ever in his words.

Manny had heard Valentino's voice in the warehouse. He'd been smooth, quiet, and confident. Not anything like he was hearing, even in those circumstances. This man wasn't Valentino. Far from it.

He spun around to Howser.

"That's not Valentino inside that house. I've heard him speak. If your men can get that man out, they need to do it now."

"Are you sure, Agent?" asked Howser.

"I am. Whoever's in there, he's not our unsub."

He took the radio from Manny. "If you can get him, commander, do it. Follow strict protocol, but we need to get him out."

"Will do, Captain. We'll—"

The sickening creak of wood weakening then letting loose from wood, followed by several simultaneous crashes, caused sparks and flames to fly high in the air.

In the next instant, even as the fire truck sirens screamed from a distance, the house caved in on itself, adding one last shower of fiery hail to the sky.

Brutal heat forced Manny, Belle, and Josh back a dozen steps into a small yard belonging to a bungalow across the street.

He glared at the burning house owned by Benjamin Grimes, feeling the tears form in his eyes as his rage climbed to new heights. Valentino had killed once again and they had been unable to stop him, once again. This freak had fooled them by going against his profile and out-thinking law enforcement.

Josh stood close, hands on hips, staring at the ground, his head shaking back and forth in disbelief.

Belle's hand slipped into Manny's and squeezed with a special intensity. He wasn't the only one entertaining the raw, disheartening frustration of helplessness. She'd put Valentino in the grave if she could find him.

Find him.

"Belle. Go find the captain or his liaison, someone, and see if you can get that picture of Grimes out to every cop in the area," said Manny as he pulled out of her grasp.

"What? Why? Oh, shit. Do you think he's still here? Oh hell, of course he is."

"Yes. He wouldn't miss this for the world. He probably thinks this is an even bigger way to show his talent and love. He wants witnesses to what he's done."

"Really? Do you think that's true?" asked Josh.

"I think it could be. We need to look for him before he has time to walk away."

"Okay. What do you want me to do?' asked Josh.

"Just start looking for him. He might even be in some kind of disguise. Maybe even dressed as a cop. I don't know, but we're wasting time. Look for someone acting strangely. A little different than the rest of the people around here."

"I'm not sure what that means," said Josh.

"You'll know if you see it." Manny pointed to his left. "You go in that direction, I'll go this way. Text me if you see him. I'll do the same. Come on, you two, get it in motion. We might have a chance to nail this bastard."

With that, Manny took off at a fast walk and began to scan the crowd, the glow from the house, along with the street lights and the police cruisers, providing him the opportunity to get a decent look at the people gathered in the area.

Quickly, he began to rule people out as Valentino. Too short. Too round. Too tall.

Each step he took led to another group of people to scrutinize, but without success.

At one point, his excitement had spiraled as he spun a young cop around because he looked like the right build for his target. But the officer had dark hair, darker eyes, and a beard. He wasn't Valentino.

When he finally reached the last taped-off area and the small group watching the house burn, he eventually had to rule out everyone in that location as a Valentino. He felt his heart sink. They had been his final hope.

He hadn't heard from Josh and certainly Belle must have delivered her message by now.

Nothing.

One more hopeful look at his phone showed no messages, only the time. Eleven o'clock on the nose.

Suddenly, he felt tired. He'd been running since early morning and had seen and felt more in a day than most people do in a lifetime. Throw in the underlying feeling of defeat, and he was ready to give it up for the day. Maybe longer. Much longer. Even when they won in this job, it felt like losing.

They had taken down Tovant, who could have gone on to worse things, but only after he'd killed cops. Hardly a consolation.

Glancing at his phone one more time, it occurred to him that Valentino had not killed in a manner that kept with his track record of even and incremental time frames.

Why? Had they messed him up by coming to the house too early, thanks to the tip from his supervisor?

That was probably it, but in the end, did that matter? The man in the house was dead.

Looking back in the direction Josh had gone, he noticed the young cop with the dark hair and beard that he'd grabbed before. He was standing alone staring at the fire, which was not unusual in itself, until he took what looked like a small pad and began to make notes. Yet, he wasn't. He appeared to be drawing.

It clicked.

Valentino had used his disguise well. He'd even changed his voice when he answered Manny's question.

This time, Manny's body stayed calm as he forced his mind and emotions to do the same. Otherwise, he'd give himself away, and Valentino would have a chance to run.

Once he reached Valentino, he stood beside him.

The officer put his pad in his pocket without hurrying, cool as cucumber.

"What a night, eh?"

"Yes sir," he answered.

There it was. That quiet, calm demeanor had escaped just long enough for Manny to hear it.

"Too bad that no-talent asshole got away."

Valentino gave him a quick look, hatred spilling from his eyes.

"No talent? No talent?"

Before Valentino could move another muscle, Manny rocked him with a right hand to the jaw, sending him sprawling to the cement. Then he was on top of him. He hit him a second time, then a third, then a fourth, feeling Valentino's nose break under his fist. He raised his hand again, then hesitated, captured by what was suddenly happening to him.

Dean's face rose from the red that filled his eyes. Then Marie's. Then the young cop who'd died on his watch. Then the six victims who had died horribly, all of them wearing Valentino's brand on their foreheads.

They were pleading for justice, for retribution, for another chance at life, questioning what had happened to them. No one wanted to give them those things more than Manny. No one. An eye for an eye. What could be better justice than that?

"Dad. Stop."

Two more faces emerged in front of the others.

Ian and Jen, their beautiful spirits rising up in the midst of the red. His children were reaching for him, their expressions holding him with such love, with such intense expectation.

How could he teach them that caring for people was what life was about, but act the opposite? His gut filled with a conflict he'd never experienced. Valentino deserved no such grace, yet Manny wasn't the man's judge.

Then Jen's and Ian's faces were gone, replaced by the scumbag who had threatened Chloe and Ian before this new nightmare had begun.

He'd shown the man mercy, even though he hadn't wanted to, and had exercised control compelled by a greater force than revenge could ever command.

It is always about the people, Williams. Remember?

Slowly, he dropped his hand to his side. He stood, pulled a dazed and bloodied Valentino from the ground, turned him around, and cuffed him.

Josh's hand rested on his shoulder.

"You got him, Manny. Now take a break," he said softly.

Then four cops surrounded Benjamin Grimes, a.k.a. Valentino, and took him in the other direction.

"Hell of a job," said Belle.

Special Agent Manny Williams walked away from his friends without answering. He wanted no accolades or anymore conversation right now.

He had something else to do and hoped he wasn't too late.

CHAPTER-42

He opened the door, pulled up a second hospital chair, and sat down beside her.

Sophie still had Dean's left hand in both of hers, rubbing it softly.

"Hi," she said.

"Hi," said Manny. "How is he doing?"

"The same. The doctors have been in a few times. They tell me the same story. He's still hanging in there, and the longer the better."

"So that's good."

She sighed. "Yeah, I suppose. It doesn't feel better. Better will be when he opens his eyes."

"I agree with you."

She shifted her gaze in his direction, her eyes red, but determined as always.

"I see you caught that son of a bitch."

"Did you get a text?"

"Yep."

"Yeah, we got him. He almost got away, but he screwed up."

"Why didn't you kill him? I think I would have."

"That's a good question. Let's just say my kids wouldn't let me."

She gave him a tired smile. "You know, I actually get that."

The door opened behind them, and Belle and Josh entered. They walked to the other side of the bed and sat in the other two chairs.

After a few minutes, Josh spoke to Sophie.

"Still the same?"

Sophie nodded.

"He is, like I told Manny. I'm not sure what that means."

"It means we still have a shot," said Josh.

"It does. The doctors also finally decided to tell me that if he makes it, he'll have only a snowball's chance in hell of walking again," she said, her emotion under control. "Did I tell you that?"

"Doctors are wrong every day," said Manny. "Let's take one step at time."

"I'm trying, Manny. I'm trying."

"I know. We all are."

"By the way, has anyone heard from Dough Boy?" asked Sophie. "I haven't been able to reach him or Barb. I think he'd like to know what's going on here."

"I talked to him via another agent. He knows. He said to tell you he's thinking of you and might even try praying," said Josh quickly.

"Okay. Thanks. I hope his prayers work better than mine and the rest of ours," said Sophie.

"It will," said Belle.

"So. I have a couple questions about Valentino and Tovant," said Sophie. "And yes, let's change the subject for a minute before I go insane."

"Have at it," said Manny.

"What was going on with those two? Josh's text said the killer was a friend of Tovant, but the pictures identifying each of them were screwed up or something?"

"It appears that Benjamin Grimes and Tovant exchanged IDs in some attempt to confuse law enforcement," said Manny.

"Why?' asked Sophie.

"It doesn't matter much now, but when the smoke clears, I think we'll find out after a little more research that Tovant was really Grimes and Grimes is Tovant."

"Explain, please," said Sophie.

"Yeah, explain," said Belle.

"Given the real Ben Grimes's personality and how the Tovant family had taken him in, I suspect he did it out of a misguided loyalty to help keep the real Eric Tovant, a.k.a. Valentino, off the authority's radar. There's no doubt in my mind, if Valentino talks, he'll reveal more murders; and the real Ben Grimes knew that. Throw in Daddy's denial and protection, and you've got a true problem."

"Really? The real Grimes would go that far?" asked Josh.

Manny shrugged. "It's not unprecedented. James Jones got over nine hundred people to drink tainted Kool-Aid. We all know that the real Grimes had mental issues, and he proved it before I took him out. I think the wildcard here is that Grimes had been loyal to a fault and tried to show that in the extreme."

"How so?" asked Sophie, her eyes wandering back to Dean.

"I'd guess he thought if he killed cops, his friend would get away with what he was doing. I don't know right now, and I don't care. We can talk about it later. Just know this was a screwed-up relationship, and neither of them is going to be able to hurt anyone again."

The fluorescent light flickered above them as five members of Manny's BAU family waited for what was next.

An hour later, the ICU nurse came in, checked Dean's vitals, readjusted one of the IV drips patched into Dean's forearm, and left after saying, "He's hanging in there." That was encouraging.

Manny watched as Sophie barely acknowledged the nurse, kissing Dean's hand again.

If ever Manny wanted God to make an appearance, it was now.

He was told once that you only had to ask God once for what you wanted Him to hear. After that, just thank Him for hearing you and let your faith take over.

He was trying, but his faith was a little low right now.

"Hey, Princess."

Manny sat upright in his chair, his eyes running to Dean's face.

Sophie's husband, his friend, and forensic tech extraordinaire looked tired, but his eyes were open and focused completely on his wife. There was a trace of a smile on his lips.

"Hey, yourself," she said.

"Did I ever tell you how beautiful you are?"

Sophie Lee held back nothing, her tears streaming down her face.

"Yeah, but I still love how it sounds, Dean."

"Good. Just know I'll always love you, okay?"

"Okay. I love you, Dean Mucus."

His smile widened. "It's Mikus, and I know that."

Dean Mikus then closed his eyes and died.

CHAPTER-43

Standing in the hospital hall, Manny relived the doctors and nurses rushing into Dean's room, yelling, prodding, and shocking Dean's chest over and over, to no avail, then emerging ten minutes later.

Dean's surgeon had taken Sophie's hand and told her they had done all they could, but Dean was gone.

The look on Sophie's face would haunt him forever.

His tough partner had been through her fair share of hell, maybe more than her fair share, but there was nothing like this one. Nothing like losing the love of your life. How could there be?

He'd held her close until she said she needed to be alone, then she wandered into the Chapel just down the hall. That was more than understandable.

Belle decided to go sit outside the chapel while Josh, after another long hug, wandered to the other end of the hall, his phone stuck to his head.

"What do we do next?"

Manny looked up and saw Josh had returned.

"That's a question for the ages, isn't it?"

"Yeah, I guess so."

"I only know what I will do next. I'm tired, Josh. I can't do this anymore. There's only so much in me. I almost killed two men this week. I'm at the end."

With that, Manny handed Josh his credentials and his gun.

"It's time, Josh. I'm leaving the FBI."

Then Manny Williams headed for the chapel to be with his friend.

Dear readers,

Thank you for reading Miami Fire. Much appreciated.

You've helped to make my dream of being a writer come true, and I thank you wholeheartedly.

Yes, Manny will be back!!

Celtic Fire is already in the works, and it will be a beauty!

What will happen next with Alex and Barb?

What of Manny's career?

How will Sophie handle Dean's death?

Who is the next threat to Manny and his family?

You won't want to miss the answers to those questions!!

Please visit me at www.rickmurcer.com or email me at rickmurcer@gmail.com

I'd love to hear from you, and I promise I will do my very best to respond to you.

If you take the time to talk to me, I'll take the time to answer.

Sincerely yours,

Rick Murcer

Books by Rick Murcer

Manny Williams Thrillers

Caribbean Moon
Deceitful Moon
Emerald Moon
Caribbean Rain
Carolina Rain
Vegas Rain
Caribbean Fire

Ellen Harper Thrillers

Drop Dead Perfect

Short Stories

The Lighthouse
Capital Murder
413
Herb's Home Run
Manny Blue and Black Max
The Killing Sands